I was happily asleep on the couch, und⸗
living room where the sun comes in. I v
ready to move quite yet. My book had f
didn't care.

Someone knocked at the door.

I ignored it. My friends would understand, and I didn't want to see anyone else. It was probably a salesman, anyway. Or someone selling a religion.

Whoever it was knocked again, louder. I wasn't parked on the street, so it couldn't be the parking guys. Aunt Agnes was in Switzerland buying dairy goats or something similar. I shut my eyes.

There was a long silence and I was sure they'd gone away.

The third time woke me again.

I got up and stumbled to the door, hot and sweaty. It was probably a good thing I'd got up. I was too groggy to be irritated. "What?"

A girl stood there, not too tall, skinny. My eyes were glared out from the sun having come through my eyelids for three quarters of an hour, and she looked green. I blinked, trying to clear them. After the third time she was still green, a delicate lime shade that wouldn't go away. I said, "Sorry, what?"

She smiled confidently. "Hi, we're in the neighborhood asking people to try out a new product."

I was about to scream and slam the door, which usually works on people like that, but I hadn't quite woken up. She really was green. She had violet eyes. I admired her for a minute, trying to think of the right response. "Really? That's amazing." I was already running out of enthusiasm. She was pretty, but completely flat chested. "What is it?"

She said, "It's the responsibility of every species to take control of their destiny."

"What?!" I recovered. This sounded dismayingly like religion, but it wasn't one I knew. That was odd, because there's something about my house that makes it attract people I don't want to see. Every guy who wants to sell a vacuum cleaner or water filter eventually winds up at my door, where he has to get in line behind people doing multi-level marketing and nuts pushing odd religions, afraid that their particular heaven may only have two or three people if they don't get their ass in gear. I average one or two a day, more if the weather is nice.

I was tempted to slam the door and pile furniture in front of it, but you don't meet green women very often, especially not pretty ones. Most of the time they're only green before they puke up all the alcohol you just paid for.

I bit the bullet. "It's pretty hot out here. Want to come inside and tell me about it?"

"Thank you. We're fairly adaptable. Could I have a glass of water?"

We sat at the kitchen table and she drank a large glass of lukewarm water. I had to show her how to use the tap, and she was baffled by the single handle arrangement.

"That's interesting. You're not quite as primitive as we thought."

"Well, we try. But where are you from?"

"About twenty thousand light years down the spiral arm towards the centre. Nobody comes out here."

"Apparently not." A trickle of water ran down her chin and she wiped it away. She was gorgeous. "But you did."

"Well, we have an interest in you. Last time we were here your planet had these horrible black creatures."

"Tarantulas?"

"What are those? Like you but smaller and hairy?"

"Monkeys?"

"Yes. We were scared that they'd become the dominant life form. They weren't very nice. We wiped them out and made a species we liked." She looked pleased with her ancestors. "Genetics."

"You killed monkeys?!"

"We didn't kill all of them. We engineered some to be more like us. We're much nicer. They wouldn't listen to any of our suggestions."

"Suggestions? Like what?"

"To be tall and not covered in hair. It seemed pretty obvious."

"So you made them like yourselves?"

"No, we made them into you. It worked."

"What?!" She was a lunatic. But she was green, so she was an alien lunatic. Maybe she was telling the truth. "When was this?"

"About six hundred thousand of your years ago. We used a lot of our own DNA, so we're very similar."

I said, using the sarcasm I'd been restraining, "You're from another star and you have DNA like ours."

"It's odd, isn't it? We think someone else went out and messed with things, before us."

"So everyone uses DNA?"

"It's popular. The Glodularians use blocks."

"Huh?"

"Blocks. Little wooden cubes with letters on them. You can't read them, of course, because they're aliens, but they can."

"So they hand each other a pile of blocks?"

"No, the male stacks them in rows, and if the female likes them she has a litter using that code."

"How long does that take? The block part, not the litter."

"Oh, about twenty-five years."

"What if there's a high wind?"

"The Glondularians are noted for their long, narrow houses."

"Huh. Why don't they make blocks that interlock? Stick together?"

"Children's toys? We sold them some, once. Half their next generation looked like lumpy racecars. It wasn't pretty."

I tried to bring this back to the original subject, but her subject was DNA and fucking with innocent species, and mine was getting her into bed. I supposed it was still all about DNA and fucking. I didn't say that. "That's too bad. But -"

She'd pulled out a brochure and unfolded it into a sheet of paper about a yard on a side. "This is what we're trying to do. Beings everywhere have let evolution get the better of them, and we're trying to teach them a better way."

The brochure was professionally done, mostly. I couldn't read the writing because it was in some type of alien script composed entirely of pillbugs in various poses. The pictures were competent, but the people in them looked subtly wrong, as though they were too enthusiastic about something they probably hated. It reminded me of communist artwork.

She was explaining something I'd unconsciously decided wasn't interesting enough to pay attention to. Her face was flushed, adding pink overtones to the green, and her eyes glowed. It was very appealing. She paused. "So you can see why someone needs to impose some order."

"Absolutely." I could see her about to start again, so I said, "But what I don't understand -" I didn't know where I was going with that, but it didn't stop her. She took off, explaining that evolution was just biological engineering carried out by random processes, and that intelligent beings could do better if you let them.

I said, "Which ones?"

"I'm sorry?"

"How do you decide who gets to do your engineering?"

She recited, "You pick the most qualified people, with the best track record, the longest history and the most satisfied customers. That's us, in all respects. We were rated number one for the last ten millennia by the Consumer Satisfaction Survey Association."

We were on familiar ground, salesman bullshit. I said, "Do you contribute money to the association?"

"Yes, and we provide them with office space. We owe it to the consumer."

"Oh." I thought again, while she talked about backpacks and unsprung weight, and the design of quadrupeds.

I said, knowing the drill, "But this is just the starter pack."

"Oh, yes. Once people see what we can do for them they're anxious to sign up for a complete species makeover."

That sounded like something you'd use to sell makeup. I wasn't sure fashion could cross interstellar cultural boundaries, or the need to match colors to green skin. I was pretty sure what they thought was a good idea wouldn't impress people on Earth, either. I was getting bored, even if she was cute. Out of the blue I said, "Do you want a drink?" She'd said they were the same as us, so it probably wouldn't hurt. "I have some beer. It's a hot day."

She smiled. "A local beverage? I should learn. I might be here for a few days."

I opened two and gave her one. She looked at the bottle as though she'd never seen one. I raised mine to my lips and took a drink.

She copied me, awkwardly. Trickles of beer ran down each side of her mouth and dripped onto her shirt, and she leaned forward and gasped. "It's cold!"

"Local custom." I drank again.

She followed. This time she didn't lose any. "It's pretty good." She drained the bottle and set it down.

I said, "Another? You can tell me about backpacks."

"Oh. Thank you. Yes." She gestured with the bottle and talked more expansively, enthusiastic.

I didn't try to keep up. After the third bottle she was quite tipsy. "This is good, and I like you. You're cute, for an alien, but that's because we made you. You don't have to thank me." She asked, "Do you think I'm cute? This stuff is okay. Can I have another one?"

I said, "Isn't that enough?"

She threw her arms around my neck. "I like you. Most planets aren't fun. I tried to sell the program to slugs. They were stupid! They don't even have vertebrae." She walked unsteadily to the fridge. "I'll get my own." She found a bottle and fumbled with the opener. "There! This is really good. Do you think I'm good looking? I don't have a lot of unsprung weight." She sat on my lap. "You're just like us. You can kiss, you're warm blooded, and you have sex. A little bit of fine tuning." She held my face between her hands and kissed me. "Mm! Nice." She unbuttoned my shirt. "Look, alien fasteners." She pulled two buttons off, but I didn't mind. I picked her up and carried her into the bedroom.

She said, "What's this? You have a special room to reproduce in. That's very sweet." She kissed me again, and she knelt and pulled down my pants. "Oh, good. Compatible equipment. We don't need the handbook."

I undressed her. She was skinny, with wide hips. Above her small waist she was almost scrawny, and she was absolutely flat-chested. I didn't mind. Her ass was round and impressive, and her upper thighs were heavy.

She lay on her back on the bed and raised her last beer to her lips. "We will engage in mock reproduction for social bonding and mutual enjoyment."

"Yes." I hoped she was right about compatibility and she wouldn't bite my head off afterwards. I lifted her legs and plunged between them. She was warm and soft, exactly right.

She smiled at me. "This is very nice. I like your planet." Her eyes unfocused for a moment. "I like you."

I moved slowly, then sped up, afraid she might fall asleep. I wasn't entirely sober, but she was much more drunk than I'd thought. It started to feel good, and then very good, and she raised her long legs and wrapped them around me. I put my hands down where her breasts should have been.

She smiled. "See? No unsupported weight." Then her eyes

widened and she sighed. "Keep doing that." She dropped her legs onto the bed so she could move with me, and she sped up, sighed, and went rigid, trembling.

I came at almost the same time, and I leaned forward over her, happy.

She rolled over, taking me with her, and I landed beside her. She said, "Nice. You can read the brochure. It's in my bag." She put her arms around me, took a deep, shuddering breath, and snored.

I got up, pulled the covers over her, wondering if aliens used covers, and went into the kitchen.

She'd left her bag on the counter. I ignored it. I'd seen enough badly printed brochures to know exactly what it would say. I sat and thought for a while. She was beautiful, but she was absolutely flat-chested. Did I want a girlfriend like that? It didn't matter. She was some odd combination of salesman and tourist, and she wouldn't be around for more than a day or two. I casually wondered what was she selling. I still wasn't going to read the brochure.

I went back to bed.

I woke up with her wrapped around me. She felt hot. Maybe aliens had a higher body temperature than us. I decided not to worry about it. Her skin was a delicate pale green against mine.

She stirred, opened her eyes and sat up. "I feel terrible. What did I drink?"

"Beer. Are you okay?"

"No." She lay down. "What's beer?" She pulled the covers over her head. "Wake me up when I'm better."

I gave her until noon, and I woke her up with coffee.

She said, "I'm a bit better. This smells good." She took a sip and screwed up her face. "It's horrible! What is this? Can I have some of the stuff I had yesterday?"

"Beer? No, it's too early. This will make you feel better."

"No, it won't. It's too awful." She handed it back to me and stretched. "Do you keep food here?"

"Yes. What do you like?"

"Qualtistats. Do you have any flent?"

"No. I don't have any of those. That. How about some toast."

"That sounds nice."

I made toast and put strawberry jam on it, and I took it to her.

She said, "This is very nice. Is it fattening?"

"You're skin and bones. You don't have to worry about that."

She looked at me, scathing. "Did you not listen to anything I said, yesterday?"

I flailed. "We were drinking beer. I was too drunk to remember, and you weren't making sense."

Her upper lip curled slightly. "You were admiring my body."

I was on familiar ground. I could handle this. "You're beautiful. I was admiring your eyes." That was true.

She relented. "Thank you. I guess you're nice." She set the empty plate on the pillow and she reached out and pulled me to her. "I feel better about this planet now I know you." She kissed me.

I reached around to squeeze her ass. It was big and round.

She bit my lower lip and said, "Do you like my body?"

"Very much." I put my arms around her shoulders and lay down, pulling her along with me.

"Good. That's a start." She kissed me again.

This time she climbed on top of me and we fucked, and she leaned down to kiss me. Her ass shook as I lifted my hips into her, and I put one hand on it and the other on her waist. Above that she was all ribs and shoulder blades, with nothing to hang onto.

She said, "This is kind of kinky. You're not really human." She kissed me again. "Go faster."

I did. She didn't match my rhythm very well, but I rose raggedly to orgasm, and I was just there when she said, "Mmm," and fell on top of me.

I lay there, holding her, and she snuggled into me. "One more time?"

"Yes."

She got on all fours and faced away from me. "This is why we're so popular."

"Your ass?" I knelt and pressed forward inside her. She felt good.

She leaned back into me. "Yes. It's so much more practical."

I didn't want another sales talk. She had a nice ass, much bigger and rounder than I'd expected, seeing her from the front. I squeezed it with both hands, and she arched her back and wiggled it. "Harder, baby. I can take it."

I went faster, and she helped, unevenly. "Do you like my ass?"

"Yes." I could still think a little bit. "It's very round."

"You're, mmm, sweet." She sighed and put her shoulders down on folded arms. "Oh."

I went faster, and a minute later I came.

After a long time she pulled away. "Get up and I'll show you some stuff."

"Sure. Just a minute." I closed my eyes.

When I woke up it was mid-afternoon, and she was holding a piece of plain bread with strawberry jam on both sides. "I made you food, but this is as close as I could find to toast."

I took a bite. "It's good." I transferred it to my other hand, pulled my housecoat in, clumsily, and followed her out to the kitchen.

She smiled. "Good. I guess you like my body."

"Yeah." The lack of tits was jarring, but she was skinny and pretty. She had a nice ass.

"Than you'll like our program. It doesn't affect men at first, but we need support."

I said, "Explain it again."

She frowned. "We made your species six hundred thousand years ago. People from our planet. We've been busy since then, but we decided it was time to send someone to check. That's me."

"You work for the people who made us?"

She hesitated. "Well, no. We're a more recent organization. They made you and left evolution to work the bugs out."

I nodded. Something wasn't exactly right, but she had a great ass. It was big by human standards, but perfectly smooth and even.

She said, smoothly, cutting into her pitch, "Evolution is a wonderful thing. It made our ancestors and provided a lot of your genetic material. But imagine how much better intelligent beings could do." Her voice became condescending and singsong. "I bet you can think of a lot of improvements."

I pictured her with breasts. I didn't speak.

She didn't care. "Our organization has redesigned people to take out those annoying natural flaws, and you can have the benefit of that work. Confidentially, we find that a lot of species are attached to the design they came with, so we're prepared to start slowly. As you can see, I'm fairly normal, but I've been improved in ways that don't show. Our organization does this as a public service, for the good of all species. Think how happy you'll be when we take the reins and leave the old random evolution where it belongs, in the mud of creation." She smiled, sure I'd bought it.

I said, "So this is a public service?"

"There are a few small charges." She spoke with the enthusiasm of the true believer. "We can't do all of the good things we do with no financing."

"But what exactly do you do?"

She looked exasperated. "It's scientific. Don't you believe in science?"

"I like to know what I'm getting into. That's not unreasonable."

"Hmph." She snorted and continued. "Evolution gave us the spine, which is an amazing thing, but it needs work. Your vertebrae are wedge shaped, like the stones in an arch, which I'm sure you've discovered, but they angle the wrong way. We've changed the angles so you're very unlikely to have back trouble, and we've redesigned the pads between them to be much tougher and more resilient." She smiled, enthusiastic again. "In addition we've lightened the upper body and moved as much of the weight off the spine as is practical."

That explained why she was so skinny. "Where does it go?"

She smiled. Onto my ass. That's why it's so nice. We've improved the shape of that, too."

I said, "It's perfect."

"Thank you. We all think so." She beamed.

A horrible suspicion was beginning to dawn on me. "And breasts?"

"There's no reason to have them unless you're nursing a baby. We make them go away until they're needed." She stuck her chest out. "I still have nipples, but the next model won't."

I said, thinking as I spoke, "So if you get fat -"

"Exactly. It all goes neatly on my hips. You want to minimize the weight your spine carries. Your hips and pelvis are ideal for that. They're the most solid part of your body."

I decided not to say that hers obviously were. She was a typical dedicated salesman with a product nobody would look at unless you browbeat them. "How many people on a planet have to buy into this?"

"Well, we'd like a majority, but you're primitives. If you'll sign the contract I'll send it in and we can get started right away." She added, "You'll get a discount. I can go to your tribal council or whatever, your village elders, but then you'll have to pay full price."

I said, trying not to panic, "I'll need a few days to think. It's not our custom to make a decision that affects everyone overnight."

She dropped back into sales mode. "No, of course not. Take all the time you want. There's no pressure. It's just such a good deal." She handed me the brochure again. "Here, you can read it if you want more details."

I said, "Thank you. I definitely will." This was the point where I'd ordinarily kiss a girl and press her into me so I could feel her breasts, but she didn't have any. I put my hand on her hip and squeezed it.

She said, "I need a few minutes. I have to file a report."

That didn't sound like a good idea. I didn't want insane aliens to make the whole human race flat chested and big assed and send us a bill. I had several old girlfriends with beautiful tits, and I might want to see them again. I had to stop her from talking to anyone. That included our elected half-wits.

"Do you want another beer while you do that?"

She nodded, absently. "Sure." When I set it down she casually upended the bottle and drank most of it.

I wasn't sure if her people had no alcohol resistance or if she didn't care. She'd taken me to bed easily enough. Earth was a sales call, but also a vacation, a place to lose your inhibitions, get drunk and have sex with someone you'd just met. I said, "What happens on an alien planet stays on an alien planet."

"Yeah. It's great." She finished her beer.

I put another one beside her.

She drank it. "You're nice."

I said, "We don't get many people from civilized worlds here."

"You should. Primitive people are fun." She slurred her words, and I was sure she wasn't hitting the right keys. She said, "I'm a little tipsy. Have to sit." She stumbled over to the couch and sat down.

I put another beer in her hand and said, "Relax. You're on vacation."

"Yeah." She drank half of it and leaned back. When her eyes shut I took it out of her hand and laid her down. She rolled over, heavily, her ass more solid than the rest of her, and she ended up facing the back, mooning me. She looked very inviting, until she twitched and started snoring. I covered her with a blanket and went back to the counter.

Her computer was still open. There was a blank rectangle full of alien hieroglyphs. The last few vertical lines were mostly the same character, as though someone had been leaning on the keyboard. She'd plugged in a mouse, and it was pretty much like ours. If you're a human being a mouse is going to have buttons and a cord.

The left side of the window had a little icon of something falling into a rippled line. Someone was throwing something into a river. Trash. The mouse was on the right side of the computer, so she was right handed, so she'd click with her index finger, like me. I clicked the river button and a bar appeared, with two buttons, one jagged and red, one a serene blue ellipse. Delete or save? I clicked the red one and the message vanished, unsent.

There was no way I could use her computer beyond that. I couldn't read the alien writing and the keyboard was completely baffling. They didn't seem to have a shift key. I wondered about aliens whose trash can was throwing things in a river and who typed everything in caps. I'd thought she was a frat girl with a crappy job, come to a planet she thought was like a drunken vacation, but maybe they were all like that.

I shook my head, trying to concentrate. Her ass stuck out from under the blanket, big and round, about at the right height. She wouldn't mind.

I concentrated on the computer.

A small black box sat next to it, connected with a green cable. That must be the connection to the galactic internet, a subspace router or something. I wondered if they had wifi.

I got my computer out and set it beside hers, and opened the top. Mine was thinner and lighter, more nicely designed. Maybe hers had a fusion reactor inside its bulky shell.

Lights flashed on her router, cycling through a rainbow of colors. They had to have software that could talk to dozens of races, refined over thousands of years for little old ladies to use. She wasn't at all technical, or I was sunk.

The lights stopped changing and went out, except for a green one. Green meant okay, because it was her skin color. Maybe.

I opened a browser. A box popped up in the lower right corner of my screen, 'New Connection found. Connect?'

I hit 'Yes,' and it said, 'Signal Strength: Excellent.'

I hit 'Home' on the browser.

It opened a page, a strange alien thing. It was polished and professional. All the graphics were impressive and didn't tell me anything. The people had pale green skin and wore dark grey and black clothes I was sure were business suits. It had the strange, amateurish look of something made by people who didn't have the budget for a proper ad agency and were sure they could do just as well.

I looked around for a button that would translate the site into English, but there were no familiar icons. They wouldn't change their web site for a market they only sent one salesman to. Probably it never got updated it all.

The galactic net must be vastly bigger than Earth's. I wondered how many worlds a civilization millions of years old had, and if their software was any good. Somewhere there was a search engine, and there had to be sites that could translate for me. My hands felt sweaty. Our whole planet could die because I couldn't find the right website.

I clicked on the close button for that tab, but they'd seen that coming and it stayed there. I was trapped by some stupid marketing executive's idea of a clever ploy. I tried the only thing I could think of, and opened a new tab, knowing it would be the same page.

It was, and a box popped up, with half a dozen alien symbols. I knew it said that access to anything but their site was forbidden.

I opened another tab, and the same page appeared. I cursed. I didn't have a hope if I couldn't get out of their little controlled area. I pulled one tab off and dropped it and the browser started another copy of itself, exactly the same as the first.

This wasn't the NSA, this was a pack of idiot aliens with a website someone's college roommate had coded. I opened another tab, and another, until I had twenty open, and the connection lagged. The last one showed a blank screen, and before it could load I pressed the little 'X' to stop it.

It stayed blank for a fraction of a second, and then the screen filled with icons, all in the same style, each a stylized image of a creature or an alien pictogram. Text scrolled across the top, ten lines of letters, icons and pawprints. I watched it go by, incomprehensible, until familiar letters went past: *Help for new species on the net.* I studied the icons, scrolling down through half a dozen screens, then back up. One jumped out at me, familiar, a tiny human outline.

I clicked it. The next page said, *Frequently Asked Questions.* I scanned it, but it was basically how to use the net. There were grammar and spelling mistakes, but someone had put a lot of work into this. I was sure the information I needed was here. I scrolled to the bottom. A big red button said, *Look Forp,* and another, *More Information.*

At the top a row of tiny red letters said, *Your Location,* and it gave me a string of numbers. I wrote them on a scrap of paper.

I clicked *Look Forp.* It had to be a search engine.

A tiny image appeared, a pretty woman with green skin. It had got our species mostly right. She was naked and had large breasts. I was delighted.

I tried to think. I entered, "Company that fixes spines."

An image appeared, a creature very much like an octopus pulling fish out of the water with twelve tentacles. It repeated every two seconds, a *Wait* icon.

The screen lit up with text and pictures. Across the top it said, *Number Of Results: Infinity.* They were all ads for back massages, and they all looked seedy.

This wasn't going to work. I put, "Companies doing business on Earth."

This time there were only ten trillion results, and none of them made sense. This was frustrating. I punched in the numbers I'd saved, carefully, and checked before I hit *Enter.*

I got five results, all press releases about the company starting a wonderful new initiative on a distant planet. The first one contained a news item about them, and the company name was blue, a link. I clicked it. Their Wikipedia logo was a slug dripping slime and smiling. I tried to figure out what that could mean, but gave up. I didn't know enough about galactic civilization. They might have millions of years of history and ten thousand worlds. Maybe that was naive, and I was off by a factor of a thousand. Even people born to their culture couldn't know a fraction of what they'd built and learned. Their Wikipedia must be the most essential thing they had.

The article was brief. It explained the company philosophy, which I knew. It listed notable successes, and they were very obviously cherry picked and exaggerated, and notable failures. They'd been investigated by someone, shut down, and there were links to the companies they'd been before they reformed in their current incarnation. They didn't give up.

A sidebar contained links to pages on the law, genocide, and cults.

I was fucked. The whole world was fucked. I pictured my batty girlfriend releasing spores or chemicals and women melting like candles above their waists, shrinking to skeletal figures with huge asses and no breasts, aliens presenting people with bills, the birth rate plummeting, the galactic police or whatever they had standing by, demanding paperwork we couldn't do.

Fuck.

I wondered about their technology. I looked up, 'Make breasts bigger.' If I was very lucky I might be able to salvage something, if I knew enough. I had their internet, but that might not help. You could know all about guns but that wouldn't save you if your enemy had them and you didn't.

I duplicated the tab and backed up to the wiki article, clicked on a link to biotechnology, and was lost in detail on the second line. I couldn't comprehend the first thing about it. I saved it as a pdf, in case we had scientists who'd like to read it as the world died.

The figure on my couch stirred and stretched, and she sat up. My heart stopped and I went to slam the computer shut, but there was no way she could read our writing. She was a tourist, not an alien anthropologist trying to understand us.

She walked over to me, rubbing her eyes, kissed me, and went into the bathroom. I heard water running, and she came back out and said, "Hello. I fell asleep. Did I send my report."

"Sure. It looked like a good one."

She smiled. "Thank you." She came over and kissed me, and then she turned and faced away, showing off her ass, and backed up into me, looking over her shoulder. It was big and soft. If nobody in your culture had tits, there'd be no point in facing someone to show off your body.

She was still a bit drunk, and that sounded like a good idea. I put an arm around her waist and pulled her over to the fridge, got out five beers and uncapped them. "Here. Our gods of hospitality will be unhappy if I don't offer you refreshment."

She said, "We can't make the gods mad." She picked one up and drank half of it. "I'm always thirsty after a presentation." She looked worried. "But when people see how great it is, they always go for it. It's very popular." She took another drink.

I said, "I'm happy you like your work."

She emptied the bottle, and another, and a minute later she was sitting on my lap, facing me. I pulled my housecoat out of the way. There was something pleasant about a girl who could sit absolutely pressed against me. I looked down her back. Her ass bulged out, enormous.

I put my arms around her, and she felt almost nonexistent, so I squeezed her hips.

She smiled and kissed me. Her beer was gone.

I handed her another, and left the fourth in easy reach on the counter.

She lifted up, slightly, slid me inside her and lowered herself onto my cock. "This is pretty nice. What do you call this stuff? Beer." She upended the bottle and swallowed until it was empty.

I moved under her, and she said, "Oh. Sex. Beer and sex." She put her feet on the floor and moved her hips up and down, and she turned that into a gentle back and forth motion, reaching over me to hang onto the back of the chair. I pumped back at her, and she rubbed her chest on mine. I grabbed handfuls of her ass.

She said, "I'm out of beer."

I leaned over and got her the last one. She kept moving.

My body took over and I started pumping harder. She emptied the beer and grabbed mine from the counter. "Can I drink yours? It really goes with sex."

She was an accomplished drinker. I'd have bet she'd just graduated from university. Theirs must be very similar to ours. "Sure. Yeah." I was breathing hard with the effort, lifting my hips towards hers with my legs, moving faster.

She set the empty bottle down and said, "Let's go for it." She bounced up and down hard, her big ass shaking. Pleasure grew inside me and I felt myself rise and overflow. I moaned and hugged her. She continued, faster, when I couldn't, and she made desperate noises, then smiled at me, relaxed and closed her eyes, and came, breathing hard through her open mouth.

"Fuck, that was good." She stood up. "I need another beer." Her speech was already slurred.

"We're out. I'll get some more." I led her into the bedroom.

She lay down on her front, her ass big and round, her torso

painfully skinny above it. She put her face on her arms and spread her legs. "I'm still available if you want me."

I knelt astride her and pushed between her legs. Her ass pressed up against my belly, big and perfectly soft. I moved slowly, and then faster. She pressed back against me, moaned and shuddered, and relaxed. She settled her face onto her arms and her breathing became steady. By the time I came she was snoring.

I wanted to lay on top of her and sleep, but I still had stuff to do. I got up and pulled the covers over her, and I dressed and went out to the kitchen and put on the coffee. While it brewed I opened my laptop.

I went back to my search. The first ten links on making breasts bigger were professional and looked expensive. That was crap. They'd screwed with us a thousand centuries back. This had to be a known field, and established technology is cheap.

The eleventh link was less elaborate, colored text with a few graphics. I clicked it and held my breath.

A page drew itself on the screen. Most of it didn't translate. There were pictures of creatures and body parts, text in a dozen languages, fifty flashing warnings. I tried to make sense of it. I opened three dozen links in new tabs, and they were all unintelligible gibberish. Some of the letters squirmed and move, almost alive. I closed them, one after another, until I was back to one page, the original.

I thought of the pale green woman asleep in my bed. Maybe I should go and fuck her and give up on this.

I sighed and looked at the page again. At the top left a small box said, "Chat with a sales agent."

I clicked it and typed, "Help."

There was a long wait. Letters appeared, one after another. "How may I help you?"

I said, "I need an antidote for breasts becoming smaller."

Another pause. "Is this a treatment you have purchased and wish to reverse?"

I tried to be clear. "A company wishes to treat my planet. This is bad."

"What is the company name?"

I went back to the wiki tab and got it, and pasted it into the chat box.

There was a pause followed by frantic typing. "These are stupid, bad beings. You are class A bipedal humanoid."

"I think so."

"A planet was treated. A friend and customer. All suffered. Wait."

I did. After a long time it typed again. "No general solution is possible without a treatment sample." A pause. "Diminution of mammary glands is your primary worry?"

"Yes." I added, "This is part of a program to fix the design or our spinal column."

"Always. Fine intentions, good mixed with destruction. I suggest this. We carry a life form engineered to cause larger breasts. A powder. This will grow itself, and may be directly ingested."

I asked, "Is it safe?"

"This is known technology. Ancient."

"How will I pay you?"

"There is no worry. They were customer, once. I will bill them."

I said, "Thank you."

"If you can strike back you must do so. Defend yourselves. This treatment is a last ditch."

"I understand."

"Good. I will express to your location. Let me check." It paused and then told me my street address.

I said, "Yes. I can't thank you enough."

"No thanks. I must leave. Another customer. Please call for all your biotechnology needs."

The box went grey. I bookmarked the site, even though it wasn't likely I'd ever get on their endless net again. I went back through my pages and bookmarked everything that looked useful before I shut the computer and put it away.

I put coffee grounds and water in the machine and turned it on. The pot filled up and I poured a mug and added milk and sugar and stood, looking out into the dark.

Everything I'd done was shaky. I'd dealt with a business that looked very fly-by-night, and they might not have anything that worked or ship it to the right address.

I didn't care. I felt strangely sure they had.

I wondered how long it would take. Would a delivery company come this far out? My green lover hadn't made an epic voyage to get here, so it must be quick. I knew I wouldn't sleep until I had the package in my hands.

I wondered if I should go and wake her up and fuck her, but I was sweaty and exhausted, as though I'd been in a battle. I sat and stared at the landscape.

An hour later I heard a noise from the bedroom. I went in and watched my girlfriend stir and sit up. I'd timed it right, and the pizza I'd ordered had just arrived.

I said, "This is hot, so be careful"

"I didn't know you could get pizza delivered way out here."

I opened a beer and put it in front of her. "Listen. We don't know each other's names. I'm Greg. You must use names."

She nodded, sucking on the bottle. "Yes, but ours are in the old language. I'm -" and she made a horrible noise of brays and squeals, like starving dolphins fighting over a wounded donkey. It went on and on.

I covered my ears.

"But my friends call me *Schkree*."

"Okay. Scree."

"Yes." She nodded. "You don't have the old language. We studied it in school. I hated it." She finished her pizza and the beer, and took another slice.

We ate, quietly. My eyes kept trying to admire her breasts, but they weren't there. She smiled back at me and wiggled in her seat, showing off her ass, even though she was sitting on it.

Lightning flashed and thunder cracked and rolled over us. Scree didn't react. Her planet had weather, too. That wasn't really a surprise.

It began to drizzle. She took the last slice of pizza and ate it. "Is there any more beer?"

"I have to go into town. I'll get some. Will you stay here?"

"Yes. I'll wait for you." She mimed kissing me.

I got my raincoat and found the keys. When I opened the door to go out to the car the sun rose, far overhead, lighting up the sky. It wasn't the sun. Something dropped from the cloud layer, a glowing, whirling device, spidery, with transparent grey helicopter blades and black insectile legs. It plummeted through the wet air, pulled itself to a stop, saw me and flew over. The blades slowed and stopped and it folded them and walked the last few feet, picking its way delicately across the wet lawn.

I stepped back and it came inside, politely. It placed a yellow plastic box, maybe a foot across, at my feet and held out a slip of paper and a pencil.

I read the invoice. "Dear customer. I have included the lichen, which will grow rapidly on rock. Also ten capsules made from the same substance, of which one should be ingested every week until the desired result is achieved. Finally our company brochure. Thank you for your business."

I took the pencil and signed where the machine indicated, and handed both things back. It tore off a small stub and gave it to me, and it bowed. It walked back to the middle of the lawn, lit up, too bright to look at, and lifted off. A moment later it was gone.

Scree said, "Anything interesting?"

I froze. She had to know what I was up to. I told myself to relax. She'd thought the pizza had been delivered from another star system. This must be a normal part of her life. "No, just a book I ordered. I probably shouldn't have." I stuffed it in the top of the hall closet and went out.

It took five minutes to drive into town, find the beer store and buy twenty cases of beer. The girl behind the till was skinny. Her name tag said, 'Scheherazade.'

She put them on a cart and hauled them outside in the rain, and she helped me load them into the trunk of the car. We both got soaked.

Her wet shirt clung to her breasts. They were nice. I missed having a girlfriend with tits.

I asked, "Is that really your name?"

"Yeah. My friends call me 'Sherry.'" She smiled, water running down her face. "Or I could be just telling you a story."

"In that case I'm sure that's what you're called."

She grinned. "Go!" She dashed back inside.

I drove home and carried them inside in six trips, and I put most of them in the basement fridge.

Scree was asleep on the bed, wearing only a t-shirt. Her ass glowed in the light coming in from the hall, round and pale. I set two beers on the bedside table in case she woke up, retrieved the box from the hall closet, and went back to the kitchen.

I tried to think. I needed a plan, because I didn't have much else.

I found an old envelope and made a list. I was sure Scree couldn't read English, but I'd keep it hidden anyway.

I wrote a title: 'Keep girlfriend from destroying the world.'

That didn't sound too daunting. Maybe. I made that the first item. 'Find girlfriend's name,' and crossed it out, so I could feel as though I was making progress. I considered adding, 'Get Scree a better name,' but that was probably impossible.

That wasn't much. I'd be fucking her a lot. I hoped I would. That was easy, and it's nice to have something on a list you can deal with. I wrote, 'Fuck Scree as much as possible.'

Under that I wrote, 'Keep Scree drunk.' So far that wasn't a problem, but I couldn't cross it off yet.

I pictured her big ass, and then her absence of tits, and I put, 'Get girlfriend tits.' Then I changed that to 'big tits,' and crossed it off.

That meant I had to do it right away.

I studied the box. One corner was slightly crushed, and there was a pattern of black smear on the side, as though something with rubber tires had brushed against it. The top opened at my touch. Four precise geometric flaps spread and folded themselves neatly out of the way.

A clear plastic bag held standard-looking pill capsules, pale transparent pink, filled with yellow-grey powder. I opened it and took out the folded sheet of paper. The top half was obviously a shipping form, done in yet another indecipherable alien script. I admired the graceful letters. Across the bottom it said, "10 capsules. Extra-potent breast enlargement, with big nipples. Dosage one per week."

Underneath that was a neat drawing of what looked like a fat centipede, rearing up and holding a pen in one long pincer. Beside it was scrawled, "Trash 'em, cowboy! Good luck! Xerxes."

I folded it and put it back.

The next item was a small plastic box full of crumbly tan sludge. Written on it in black felt pen was, "Lichen. Instructions: Scrape onto a rock."

I tiptoed back to the bedroom and looked in. Scree lay on her front, her ass sticking appealingly up in the air. I hesitated for a minute, but duty called me.

I took a butter knife and the plastic box and went quietly out into the front yard, making sure the screen door closed silently behind me. The house had come with a half dozen boulders, the biggest of which was five feet tall. They made it impossible to cut the lawn, so someone had planted shrubs all around them, and by now they were chest-high.

I waded through the vegetation until I was between the front of the house and the largest boulder. The box popped open easily. I picked up a dab of lichen and smeared it onto the rock, and I did all five of them, putting it where they'd be shaded for most of the day. There was still lots in the box. I snapped the lid down, carefully, and went inside.

Scree was lying on her back, snoring. I pulled the covers over her, and waffled for a moment over whether to get under it with her. I still had one more thing to do.

I got a beer out of the basement fridge and held it, wrapped in a cloth on my workbench, and popped the cap off with a screwdriver. I'd forgotten the pills. I sneaked quietly upstairs, looked in on Scree, took the box down to the basement and emptied one pill into the bottle. Then I pressed the cap back on and made a tiny mark on it with a felt pen so I wouldn't get the wrong one. I put it right at the front of the upstairs fridge. I had a plan. It might even work.

I opened my computer and got onto the galactic net. I'd left the browser open and when it tried to take me to the corporate website I opened three tabs, crashed one, and clicked on the wiki link.

So far as I could tell, the only difference between us and these lunatics was that they could get onto the galactic net, and they had starships. I searched 'star drive,' and 'faster than light,' 'warp drive,' and 'subspace.' I found a hundred billion links to what looked like old TV shows, except the humans were aliens and the aliens were other aliens in rubber suits. They looked terrible, maybe worse than Earth TV.

I tried everything I could think of for half an hour, but there was too much to wade through. Finally I tried 'car.' That finally got me spaceships, rockets, saucers, globes, endless hits, most of them company pages, reviews, and advertising. I admired the flashy sports models and got lost in technical specs, but I didn't want to buy one. At least I couldn't afford it.

One link was a page about doing your own repairs. A large smiling alien wielded a massive wrench and lifted an exotic engine out of a red ship the size of a semi-trailer. His site had a link to another one, where ropy aliens rebuilt equipment I couldn't identify. They referenced a page which listed the most common starflight systems and how they worked. I tried to save it as a pdf, knowing it wouldn't work, but it did. An hour later I had the theory behind two dozen drive systems, instructions on how to build them, and a manual on how to line the back of a starship with shag rug and install a bed. At the end the author, who looked like a Yeti, sat on his creation with the female he'd built it to seduce. She was cute.

I wrote, "Steal alien technology' on the list and drew a line through it. Then I went back and found an explanation of their faster-than-light internet, downloaded it, and saved it with a reasonable file name. It probably required fields of technology it would take millennia to develop, but it was worth a try.

I felt I was making good progress, even if nothing I'd done put off the threat of a world-wide boobs catastrophe. I wondered if there was some kind of galactic police force. Then I pictured the guys who ran speed traps out on the main road being in charge of the whole galaxy. I decided to handle this myself.

I took the two beers I'd left out back to the fridge, and put the one I'd marked on the bedside table with the cap still on. Then I undressed and slid over next to Scree, under the blankets. She was warm and, below the waist, cuddly.

I watched her carefully the next day, and the one after that, worried that the pill I'd given her had been useless. Nothing happened.

I kept her slightly drunk, which wasn't difficult, and we fucked, and she slept on the couch and in the sun. When she looked restless I taught her to drive my car on the back roads where there was never any traffic, and we made love in the back seat. I told her it was an old Earth custom, which I realized later was true.

She said, "I can't imagine who thought of this. It's so cramped." She leaned forward and kissed me. "It's kind of fun, though."

In the evening we cooked steaks over an open fire in the back yard. She was amazed. "I thought this was a myth, but you can really do it." I sent her back to the house for beer, four times, so I could watch her ass wobbling away. She drank them and sat on my lap on the grass, naked.

I hugged her and was almost sure her chest wasn't just ribs any more. I kissed her where they should have been, but I couldn't tell.

She said, "That's sexy," and pushed me over backwards on the grass.

Three days later, we were sitting on the couch, making love, and she was bouncing up and down on my lap. She said, "Huh?" and looked down. She stopped, and gave another tentative bounce. Her small breasts jiggled.

She said, "I don't have -" and bounced again. They shook, like little mounds of jelly. She breathed, "Oh. Fuck," and did it harder. Then we were moving fast, passionately. She said, "Kiss my boobs."

They were barely big enough, but when I did she came, panting and bouncing, and I did, too.

After that she was blossomed wonderfully. When we weren't fucking I did some math in my head. I'd hoped I could make her too big for her cult, but even if she grew an inch a day I'd have to keep her on the stuff for a while. If she was about a thirty, now ... a week was thirty seven, which is nice but not huge. Two weeks was bigger, forty-four. That wasn't enormous, and she could hide it if the other people in her cult were idiots. That was a possibility. I realized the fate of the world depended on how well I could do this. It would have to be three weeks. Shit. Could I keep her drunk vacation going for twenty-one days? I decided I could. It might even be fun.

The next day she looked down at her chest several times. I wasn't ready for her to realize she was getting bigger, so I said, "Tell me again about your program."

She immediately dropped into her talk, ignoring distractions like the small bumps sticking out through her shirt. "Our original design wasn't that good. The old ones made us from quadrupeds, and our upper body isn't built to carry a load. You see, your spine is flexible, and all the support for your shoulders is done with muscles. There aren't any nice big ball joints like in your hips. It takes energy to carry weight high up, but none if it's on your hips."

I said, hoping I wouldn't regret it, "If it can't be high up, why don't you design people with fat legs?"

"Unsprung weight. You can't make the parts you have to move while you walk any heavier. Your hips are the ideal place."

"Oh. Well, that makes sense."

"Yes, it does." She came and sat on my lap, facing away from me.

I lifted her up, and she reached between her legs and positioned me, and I let her down onto my cock. She wiggled her hips and eased down into place. Her ass was big and round, larger than it had been when she'd come to my door. Days of takeout food and beer were having their effect on her.

She moved up and down, slowly. "Ready to sign, yet? All your women could be like me, and our old ones would be happy, if they knew."

She'd faced away from me so I could admire her ass. This was a strange mixture of drunk sex on vacation and a sales presentation. I put my hands on her hips and squeezed them. I said, "It's certainly on my mind."

"Usually if a planet signs up they'll be offered membership in the galactic federation. We generally give new members drive technology. Governments like that a lot."

I knew that was crap. If there was a galactic federation it wasn't any more impressed by these deranged traveling salesmen than I was. I was pretty sure their old ones didn't carry much weight with anyone outside their cult. "I'm sure that would be very useful." I put my hands up and found her breasts. They were decidedly bigger.

"That's nice." She moved slowly, rocking her upper body sinuously back and forth. "My superiors have suggested that I go directly to your government." She leaned forward and gasped, "You've made some evolutionary mistakes, and we need to get you back on the true path." Then she was panting and trying to move, suddenly uncoordinated. Her last statement worried me, but I took over and thrust hard, shaking her, and I slowly started to feel very good, and I sighed and exploded into her.

She got up. "That was really nice."

I said, "Once I sign your contract you'll have to go back to your headquarters. I've really enjoyed having you here. It's like a vacation."

She smiled at me. "Maybe a few more days. I'm having a good time, too." She went to the fridge and got herself two cans of beer. "I love your planet."

She didn't say she loved me. I already knew I wasn't a romantic encounter, just a convenient fling in a vacation spot. I didn't mind. She had a great ass, even if it was getting a bit large, and nice small breasts.

I asked, "Your old ones. Where are they now?"

She drained one beer and opened the next. "The old ones left and went somewhere else. They said they'd be back in a few days."

"How long ago?"

"About twelve thousand years."

"I think you can give up on that one."

"Well, we want to be ready. Streamlined."

I didn't point out that her ass wasn't at all streamlined. I might not ever get laid again. I said, "Come here."

"Okay." She upended the second beer and drank.

I led her into the bedroom, wondering if all of her people had her amazing talent for consuming beer, and she lay down on the bed. I put my hands up and felt her breasts, then moved them to her ass, worried that I might draw too much attention to them. I rolled her over on her front so they wouldn't bounce.

She spread her legs. "Hang on, I'm not comfortable." She squirmed her chest back and forth.

I said, "Here," and handed her a pillow. "Put this under your shoulders. You're probably not used to our primitive mattresses."

She settled onto it. "That's better. Do you like my ass?"

"It's glorious." It pressed up into me as I fucked her, big and round.

I thought I was going to get another sales lecture, but she said, "Good," and relaxed, closing her eyes. "Go slowly. I'm a bit lazy."

I did, and she didn't move. Once I was sure she was asleep, and I slowed down, but she moved her hips and murmured, "Don't stop." After a few minutes her breathing deepened and sped up, and she shifted slightly and angled her hips up at me. "Slowly, baby." She relaxed again, and her breathing slowed. She was wet inside, and soft.

I kept going, trying not to let the slow heat inside me take over, but my body glowed and burned. Scree sighed and moved under me, lifting her ass into me. That changed everything, and I couldn't slow down. She angled her hips from side to side, then arched her back, and said, "Oh. Mm." The muscles in her back tensed, and she lifted her hips off the bed, and I came, thrusting into her over and over, trying not to let it end.

She slowly sank back onto the mattress. "Baby, I've never come like that. That was amazing."

I said, "Yeah. It was. Primitive planets have that effect." I wondered if it was from having breasts. I didn't want to say that.

"Would you like a beer?"

"Well, they're awfully nice, especially after sex."

I got us one each. I'd doctored hers earlier in the day, and I was afraid she'd notice the taste, so I said, "It's a new type. Tell me if you like it."

She took a sip. "Yeah. It's really good." She drained the whole bottle. "Will you be mad if I get drunk and lie in the sun?"

I said, "What happens on alien planets stays on alien planets."

She smiled and rolled over. "Yeah." She pulled me to her and kissed me. "You're the best primitive lover ever."

The next day she was hung over. I took her breakfast in bed, and a beer, which she drank. Then she rolled over and went to sleep, leaving everything uneaten but a slice of toast.

In the afternoon she moved to a deck chair in the shade, and I kept her supplied with beer, which she sipped, and she went through half a dozen cans by nightfall.

I asked her about her home world, and she said, "I can't discuss business right now. I may be dying."

She went to bed at eight, and I lay cuddled up to her, against her soft ass. When I was sure she was asleep I let my hand drift down her chest and I cupped her right breast. It filled my hand, delightful. I squeezed it, unable to stop. She muttered something and shuffled her ass back into me.

In the morning she woke before me. I heard her inhale sharply and the bed shifted. I knew she was feeling her breasts. She walked quickly into the bathroom, and I watched her, pretending to be asleep.

She came back, upset, holding them. "What's this?! What the fuck is going on?!"

I sat up, alert. "What?" I'd been trying to think of an answer to this for days, but all that came up was being innocent. "What's wrong?"

She said, "My boobs. They're enormous. What the fuck?"

I said, "Let me see them."

She dropped her hands. "There."

They were perfect, large breasts. "They look okay to me. Do they feel swollen or something?"

"They're huge! I wasn't this big when I came here. I'm supposed to be tiny." She was having trouble controlling her lower lip, and I knew she was about to burst into tears.

I said, "Doesn't this happen on your world? Women often wake up with big tits. All the time." I tried to think of an explanation she'd buy. They had their old ones, who they treated as sort of gods. "We think it's the will of the Bubinga tree gods. Their pollen."

Her eyes overflowed and she sobbed, "No. Nobody told me."

I leaned forward and raised her face, wet with tears, so I could see her violet eyes, and I gently kissed her lips. "You're even more gorgeous. I want you."

She threw her arms around me and kissed me, and the next few moments were a flurry of arms and legs and clothing being torn off.

We fucked, frantically, until we were sweaty and exhausted, and when I came she wasn't far behind me. It was glorious. I didn't have enough hands for her tits and her ass, but I squeezed her and kissed her breasts, and she arched her back and pressed my face into them. She moaned and writhed and hugged me, hard, and this time her breasts squashed between us, big and soft.

Afterwards I sat beside her on the couch, with one arm behind her, in the space above her big ass, and we slowly lay down together. I could feel myself drifting off. I had to get up and get her some beer, but the day was warm and bright.

I woke with a start. She was gone.

I pulled on my pants and dashed outside. She was probably spreading whatever lunacy she'd brought. I realized that if she was successful the pool of women I'd find sexy was exactly one, and she was an insane alien.

She stood sixty feet away, under the big trees behind the house, naked, with her arms above her head and her legs spread. Her skin glowed brilliant green in the sunlight. "Tree gods, give me bigger boobs! I beseech you!" She held a beer can in her right hand and was quite drunk.

I walked up and put my arms around her. Her breasts were just more than handful, soft, her nipples hard.

I said, "If you want something from the tree gods they need a sacrifice."

She turned and hugged me. "What?"

I took the beer from her hand and upended it over the lawn. "Oh great trees, grant this woman the favor of your bounty. Make her breasts large and firm!" I tossed the can back towards the house. "Now we have to fuck. That's important."

She put her arms around my neck, drunkenly seductive. "I like your planet."

I pulled her down onto the grass. It wasn't like I had any close neighbors. The grass was cool, but she didn't mind. Her breasts wobbled back and forth on her chest and her big ass lifted her hips into me, and I rose to climax and came.

When I looked down she was smiling and had her eyes shut. I half-carried her into the house and put her on the bed. She rolled over and started snoring.

I got a big glass bowl, filled it with ice, and put four beers in it. I left it on the bedside table. Then I went out and fired up my computer. She'd left herself logged on, and in two minutes I was on the galactic net. It was time to do some more research.

She didn't wake up until the next day. I watched her sit up, stretch, and grab her breasts with both hands. She looked happy, and smiled at me. Then her eyes widened and she looked scared. "Did I really pray to your gods yesterday?"

"Yes." I didn't say that she'd drunkenly given half a beer to a stand of pine trees. It didn't sound as impressive. I handed her a can.

She looked pleased. "Beer? For me?"

"We always do that for visitors."

She grabbed one, popped the top, and guzzled half of it. "Your world is easier to deal with if I have a beer inside me." She looked down at her tits. "Fuck."

I sat beside her and cupped both of them. Today they filled my hands and solidly overflowed them. She looked very sexy. I said, "Want to fuck?"

"Let me do something first." She drained her beer and picked up another, drank half of that and went into the kitchen. I lay back and close my eyes, but I had to know what she was doing.

I looked outside.

She stood on the lawn, still naked. She said, "Oh trees, keep doing that. Here's a beer. I'll lay your boy now." She tipped the beer, stopped and held it to her lips, drank what was obviously most of it, and poured the last couple of ounces out on the lawn. Then she burped and walked determinedly back to the house. Her breasts wobbled and she ignored them.

I took her in my arms and pulled her down into bed.

The next morning her breasts were bigger. I saw her all the time, so it was hard to estimate how much they were growing, but within a week they were huge. I woke to find her standing in front on the mirror, looking aghast. At first she'd cupped them in her fingers, then mostly supported them, but now they bulged hugely out of her hands. "Baby, this is getting scary. I need a decision on the deal." She didn't even tell me how great it would be.

I said, "The elders are working on it. Just a few more days." I grabbed her from behind and kissed her neck. Her breasts felt enormous. I squeezed them and she pressed her heavy ass back into me.

I said, "I think we need some beer and leftover pizza. Today is the festival of Ra, and we need to -" I tried to think, and ended lamely with, "do those things. And fuck."

She said, "Okay, baby." She drained two beers, desperate to be buzzed and not worry about her mission. When she pulled her shirt on it wouldn't do up. She tried to pull the front together, squashing her breasts, but they were too big and firm, and they stuck proudly out, round and pointed. I couldn't have covered her nipples with teacups.

She looked worried.

I said, "Baby, it's the festival of Ra. I've already had six beers, you have to keep up. Here!" I handed her another.

That was crap, but she smiled. "I love this primitive shit. It's so authentic. I could stay here and be so natural." She'd given up buttoning the shirt and her breasts stuck out, half concealed by the loose fabric. She leaned back to drink half the beer and they rose up and pointed at me.

"Stay there." I dug through my closet. When I'd lived in the city I'd gone to a costume party and I'd bought a dozen grass skirts for my friends. I was sure I still had them.

She sat and watched, looking at me over her breasts. Every so often she'd glance down at them, surprised.

I found the skirts in the third box. I pulled one out, tore off the plastic and the cheaply printed cardboard header, cut my thumb on a staple, sucked it, cursing, and said, "Festival clothing. You have to wear this." I tried to think. "But Ra isn't like the trees. You have to have big boobs."

She looked proud and hurt. "I *do* have big boobs." She pulled the skirt on and settled it into place on her hips. Her ass stuck out through the strands of grass, big and round.

I looked at them, critical. "Baby, Ra is a very selective god. I'm afraid he'll think they're kind of little. All the temple acolytes have big ones."

She held them again, accidentally mashing her beer into the right one. "Ooh. That's cold. I thought they were big." She sounded hurt.

I led her out into the front room. It was cloudy, but I could see it breaking up. I said, "Here. Drink this." I handed her another beer.

She emptied it. "Okay."

I said, "Now say, "Ra, I want to have big boobs. Please favor me." She repeated it.

I waited, and the moment stretched on. Just when I was about to give up the sun burst through the clouds, lighting up the room, and her body.

I said, "Ra has decided. You're okay."

She said, "I never thought it would be like this." She waved her empty can and swayed. "What do we do now?"

I caught her, and she leaned against me, squashing her breasts into my chest. I said, "We have to drink a lot of beer. Beer is sacred to Ra."

"Okay." Half an hour later she was leaning back in a lawn chair, snoring.

She woke up two hours later, and walked unevenly into the house to admire herself in the bathroom mirror. She came out with a can of beer and danced in the sunlight, her breasts bouncing. "Ra loves me! I have big boobies, and nobody else has, and soon all your Earthie girls will be efficient and flat." She emptied the beer and bent over, heavily, to set the can on the grass. "Come and fuck me. Ra, you can watch!" She spread her legs and tilted her head back.

I stripped and took her. When it was over we slept, side by side in the sun.

Scree was increasingly on vacation. She drank and lay in the sun and didn't talk about the contract. She'd wake up, guzzle a beer, and we'd talk, and she'd sleep. I fucked her over and over. There was something about her superior attitude and swelling breasts that made me want her all the time, and she happily obliged. I was sure that what happened here was so far from her real life that it didn't feel real to her, and didn't matter. I was pretty sure she just wanted to get drunk and laid away from the repressive and bizarre society she'd have to go back to.

On a Thursday morning she sat up, drank half her beer, and put it down. "I need to go and check in at base. It's the weekly meeting."

"Really? You haven't finished your beer."

She absently drained it. "Where are my clothes?"

That was a problem. She wasn't just busty, she was enormous. Twin fat cones stuck out in front of her, pale green with the faintest pink overtones. They were gorgeous and overwhelming, as wide as her shoulders, and they stuck hugely out in front of her, perfect pointed ellipses, far too big for her skinny chest.

She pulled on her shirt and they angled back and forth as she moved her shoulders. I watched, stupefied.

She left it open and bent down to pull up her pants. Pointing at the floor they looked even bigger, and she stumbled, one leg caught in the fabric, and almost fell. I caught her, getting a handful of one breast. It was nice.

She pulled away and yanked her pants up. They were painfully tight over her thighs, and her ass bulged out of the back. She exhaled and barely managed to pull the fly closed. "Shit." When she took a deep breath the fabric creaked. She tried to pull the shirt closed over her breasts, but they were far too big. She managed to squash them far enough to get one button done up, but it looked ridiculous and made the others impossible. She looked down, horrified. "I have a meeting. I can't go to it like this. What can I do?"

I hugged her, and as I spoke I undid the button, pulled down her fly and undid the waist. "It's just a meeting. You're out on an assignment, and you got hung up." I pulled the pants down and said, "There. Is that nicer? Baby, people often gain a bit of weight on vacation." I leaned over and kissed her neck, and I put my hands on the bulges where her hips pulled in to her waist. "You'll lose that in two days when you get back." I kissed her on the lips and held a huge breast in each hand. They didn't remotely fit. "You're still on vacation until we can get this thing sorted out, right? Here, take your pants off and I'll get another beer. You can write to your home office and tell them you're sorry but you'll definitely be at the next meeting. Everyone loves a good meeting, but they understand if you miss one." I knelt and kissed her breasts, and I sucked each nipple, just for a minute.

She sighed. "Okay. That's nice. I hadn't realized."

I pulled her pants down the rest of the way and she stepped out of them. I leaned forward and pressed my face into her breasts again. "Come on. Pretend you're one of us primitive people." The sun shone through the windows. "Look, Ra is shining to tell us he likes your boobs."

She walked to the window and raised her arms. Her breasts stuck out further than she thought and they pressed against the glass. I vowed never to wash it again.

She said, "Thank you, Ra. I'll make them bigger if the trees will help."

She walked past me and into the kitchen, drained a beer, and continued onto the back lawn, her breasts bouncing with each determined step. "Trees! Make me bigger. Ra demands it, and he gets a longer festival than you!" She upended the can and watched the last few drops drain out, threw it into the bushes, and lay on her back. "Come and fuck me. I need to feel better."

I enthusiastically did, and we lay under the hot sun, sweaty and oozing cum. I decided moments that good weren't common, so I went and got four beers out of the fridge.

She lay on her back and drank, spilling it all down one cheek. After the second one I climbed up onto her and spread her legs with my hands.

"Hey! I'm trying to drink."

"The trees don't like it if you just lie there. We have to. They might do something awful."

"Like what?"

I whispered, "Like making your pants too small."

"Oh." She asked, almost inaudibly, "Do you think?"

"Yes. We'd better hurry."

She nodded, raised the can and drunkenly poured half a beer over her face. She laughed. "Shit. Trees, that was for you!" Then she whispered, "Kiss my boobs. It feels nice."

That afternoon she slept on the couch and I drove into town. I filled the trunk with beer, and drove to the second-hand store, took her pants in and asked the woman who worked there to find a bigger pair.

She looked at me as though I was an imbecile, then said, "Got it." We went through stacks of clothing stuffed into shelves taller than either of us, and found a pair she said would probably do. I couldn't tell them from the originals.

I left Scree's old pair and paid for the others, and I picked out a big, formal shirt and bought that, too.

She smiled and said, "I think you're very nice to do this for your girlfriend."

I didn't explain.

I got two pizzas and took them home with me, and I put the pants on her floor where I'd picked up the other ones. Then I stuffed the fridges with beer, and opened a pizza.

"Hey. Wake up. I got some different beer."

She opened her eyes and stood up, gloriously naked. "Oh. Did I sleep long?"

"Half an hour." I opened a pizza box. "Here, native food. With pineapple."

She picked up a slice. "This is really good. I shouldn't be eating so much."

"You're on vacation." I picked up the pants. "Try these on again, now you're more relaxed."

I knew that didn't make any sense, but she pulled them on, stopped to look at the tag, and shrugged. They slid into place, comfortably loose. She smiled. "Oh. That's better."

"See." I'd left the shirt on the counter. "One of my old girlfriends forgot this here. Do you want it?"

"Sure." She slipped it over her shoulders. It didn't disguise the sheer volume of her breasts, but it covered them, light and airy. She sighed. "I guess I was upset about nothing."

"You'd just woken up." I took another slice of pizza. "You look gorgeous."

"Thank you. This is nice beer."

"I got lots. Primitive people like beer."

She said, "So what's the next festival?"

"Cindy, the goddess of milk and lingerie. And boobs."

"What do we have to do?"

"Fuck, eat pizza, and have big tits." I added, "All our gods are alike." I pretended to study her critically. "But Cindy's a bit less forgiving than the trees. If we're going to do this you can't keep covering them up."

She looked worried. "Is at night okay?"

"Of course. She likes big ones, and she likes beer, but you have to drink it for her."

She took a long drink of hers and kept tilting it up until she'd emptied it. "I can do that." She opened another.

Half an hour later I'd finished my beer and had four slices of pizza.

She said, "I'm quite drunk. I hope your Cindy is happy."

"You should probably let her see your boobs."

She nodded and weaved her way to the front door, undoing her shirt. When she was outside she pulled it off and stuck out her massive breasts. "All you Earth gods! Here they are? Are they big enough?" She added, "I can make them bigger. No, you can. Do it!" She shut her eyes and screwed up her face, as though she was about it be hit by breast-shaped lightning.

I grabbed her and pulled her into me. "Did you feel that? I nearly fell over. Was that an earthquake?"

She hugged me and cuddled into me, pressing her breasts against my chest, half sideways. "No, that was the touch of the divine. Your gods like me because I'm civilized." She shivered. "I think I'm bigger."

"They want us to fuck."

She said, "But I just got my pants on."

"I think those pants were a gift from the gods. Maybe Ra."

"Oh." She fumbled with the fly and pulled them down. "Oh. Fuck me, then."

I did, lying on my back the lawn, with Scree on top, bouncing up and down, her breasts shaking until I took them in my hands and steadied them. They were too big to hold, but I managed, and she moved faster until she came.

She stopped, sighing. "Fuck, I love this planet."

I hadn't come yet. I held onto her breasts, keeping her in place and kept moving until I was suddenly overwhelmed and I came. She slumped forward into me, already half asleep, her breasts huge and awkward between us.

I lay and watched the stars for a long time, until I was cold, and I rolled her off and walked her into the house. She sat on the couch and looked sleepy. She lifted her breasts and looked amazed, as though she'd never seen them. "Baby -"

I was out of answers, so I gave her another beer and said, "I think Cindy wants you to drink this." Five minutes later she was snoring. I carried her the short distance to bed. She wasn't as light as I expected. She hadn't had such a big ass when she'd come here, or huge tits.

From then on I brought her beer in the mornings, fucked her over and over, as often as I could, provided her with takeout food and made up primitive religious festivals: Grool, god of beer and big tits, Tria, the insanely busty goddess of pizza, Tanya, goddess of sex and nudity, who had big breasts, and Ed, god of debauchery and drunken sex, who was always accompanied by his acolyte Babs, who bestowed enormous tits on women she liked.

Scree switched between yelling, "I have such great tits," and drunken sobbing at least twice a day. I fixed it with alcohol and takeout food and sex. I was sure she didn't care about the contract any more, she just wanted something to take back to explain how she'd got so enormously busty. Her tits stuck out, enormous, ungainly and erotic, too big to be real, and each day they were bigger.

I did research on line at night, and I downloaded reams of information about Galactic culture. If I could pull this off we'd build starships and contact someone who wouldn't destroy us, and it would all be trivial. I didn't dare stop. When I went shopping I bought bigger pants and shirts at the junk shop, and I swapped them out when hers looked tight.

Every Sunday I went outside at dusk and scraped a teaspoon of lichen off the rock and put it on her food. Her tits grew enormous, then titanic, impossible.

In the evening of the twenty-eighth day I fucked her in the long grass under the trees. Her breasts swayed back and forth under her, round and perfect.

She said, "The long grass tickles."

"You're not -" The grass needed to be cut, but it wasn't all that long. Her breasts hung down far enough to touch it. They were gloriously huge. I said, "Yeah, me, too."

When we were done she struggled to her feet, so amazingly busty that she'd become unsteady. She giggled and rubbed her breasts into me. "Baby, it's like growing another set of hands. I want to feel you all over with my boobies."

I rolled over onto my back. "I think you should do exactly that."

They were big and awkward, and it took a long time. I lay and enjoyed every minute, and then she lay down in the grass and we made passionate, slow love. She leaned up and rubbed them into my chest again, saying. "This is the best thing ever. Kiss me, baby."

When she came she arched her back and they pointed up at me. I bit her nipples, gently, and she shook and closed her eyes, moaning.

We stumbled into the house, exhausted and drunk, and we fell into bed.

I studied her in her sleep. It was hard to tell, because I'd been looking at her for so long, but I knew she was far too big to sell women on the merits of being flat-chested, or to explain to the people in her cult why she hadn't.

I knew our time was nearly up.

On the twenty-ninth day she stood up, stretched, and fell over forwards. "Oh, fuck. What have I been doing?" She looked up at me. "This is your fault. You and your fucking planet."

I said, "Come and lie down. You look nice."

"Fuck you." She tried to get up, fell over again, and struggled to her feet, clinging to the bed frame. "Oh. What am I going to do?"

I got her a beer. "Relax and let's think."

She drained most of it. "What happens on alien planets stays there. Shit. This won't. Look at my boobs. I can't be like this. Everyone knows this is wrong."

I said, "I don't think so." I reached out and squeezed them both. They were amazingly big and soft.

She said, "Mm. Stop that." She leaned into my hands, lost her balance and grabbed the bedpost. "This is your fault, baby. What can I do?"

She looked lost and innocent, not the pushy saleswoman who'd come here. I said, "Hang onto that." She did, and I stood behind her and stuck my cock inside her.

She said, "Stop! I have to go! What are you doing?" After a few minutes she relaxed. "Can you reach my boobs, baby? Kiss me."

Ten minutes later she came, clutching the bedpost, orgasming so hard that the frame shook.

I watched her euphoria fade away, leaving misery and anger. "Look at me, I've got huge boobs and my shirt doesn't fit. What will the bosses think?" She broke down and sobbed, "What have I done? This is your stupid planet. Look how big I am." She spat, "You lied to me. You just wanted an easy fuck! You were never going to sign, and now look at me! How can I go to our next progress meeting with these stupid things? Nobody will want to come here, and you'll be all alone and all your women will have tits! I'll think about you and laugh at them." She pulled herself upright, turned her back on me, and knelt down to stuff clothing that didn't fit her into a bag.

Under one pile was a small pink device with a red button. She pressed it. "There. My ship's coming to get me, and I'm leaving. You'll never see this ass again, and I'll never fuck you."

I said, "Do you want another beer?"

"Yes. Asshole."

She drank three more, and she sobbed again. "What's wrong with your stupid planet? It's done this to me. I'll never get to the next level now. We're not supposed to have *these*." She picked up the company shirt she'd worn when I first met her, and tried to pull it on, but it wouldn't close over her breasts. She angrily pulled up the last pants I'd bought her, a week ago, but they wouldn't zip up. The grass skirt I'd given her stuck out from under the bed, and she picked it up and stretched it over her wide hips. "I need a top."

I pulled an old jacket out of the end of the closet. I hadn't worn it in years. She pulled it on and left the front open. She looked extremely odd, but sexy, and very angry.

I got her another beer and carried her bag, and we went and sat on the front steps.

Five minutes later a dot appeared in the sky, almost too far up to see. It dropped fast, and I could make out more details. It was a perfect, classical flying saucer, painted hot pink, with delicate chrome trim around the portholes and the door. I wanted one, desperately.

It slowed and landed in the middle of the driveway. The door opened and a ramp extended down to the ground.

I said, "We could make out before you go."

Scree stood up. "You primitive alien asshole! I'd have given you the star drive. Now what do you have?" She hiccupped and her breasts bounced. She clutched them and clumsily walked to the ramp. "I'm going to Washington to give it to them. They'll sign the agreement. Before you know it there won't be a busty woman on your planet and I'll be two levels higher and I won't sleep with your primitive ass!"

I said, "I gave it to them."

She turned pale. "You don't have it."

"I downloaded the plans while you were drunk. I logged on through your router."

"You're lying! Primitives don't have networks."

"Then go to the government and see how fast they toss your drunk alien self in prison. They'll probably keep you for about fifty years until they're sure you're not a threat."

"Asshole! I should bomb you from orbit."

"Baby doll, people who go door to door don't have weapons, or they wouldn't be going door to door. All you've got is tits. Nice ones." I added, maliciously, "And a bit of a big ass."

She looked down at her ass, tried to think of something cutting to say, sneered at me, and walked up the ramp, angry and dignified, her head held high. Her breasts stuck out of the jacket like green icebergs, delicately shaded in pink. When she got to the top she stopped and said, haughtily, "Your religion is completely stupid. It sounds as though it was made up on the spot." She added, scathingly, "By an idiot." She tried to slam the door, and her breasts, sticking out of the jacket, wobbled hugely. The door closed itself smoothly on silent pneumatic cylinders.

I looked at them. They were like the ones that had held the hatch on my last car open, except they'd been worn out and you had to prop it up with a stick. I didn't care. We could build spaceships like this. Our own saucers. If I sold the plans to a big corporation I could get a flashy one.

I expected the ramp to retract, but the saucer sat, unmoving. I sneaked up and looked in through one of the window.

Scree was passed out in the pilot's seat. I could have gone inside and taken her keys, but there's a good time to end a relationship, and this felt like that point. I went back inside and got the lichen, mixed it with some water and a bit of honey to make it sticky, and smeared it on the landing skids. Then I sat on the porch and waited.

Half an hour later she woke up, made an alien but obviously insulting gesture through the window, and took the controls. She didn't look at all competent or awake. The saucer rose unevenly into the sky until it was too small to see, the ramp hanging down from the doorframe, forgotten.

I was relieved when Scree was gone, but also, unexpectedly sad. The house felt empty, and there was nobody to drink with, to make love to at odd hours, and to make up strange religions for.

I waited all afternoon to see if she came back, and that turned into days. I cleaned up and slept, made a few meals, tried to get drunk by myself and found it wasn't fun, scraped lichen off the rocks into food storage containers and put them in the deep freeze.

When the weekend came I went out to a bar. I didn't meet anyone wonderful. There were cute girls, but none of them had Scree's exaggerated body and her enormous breasts.

For the next week I thought about that, but mostly I watched for her saucer coming back, or for an invasion of her co-workers. When I went into town I studied the girls on the streets to see if their shirts looked empty. I read the news, looking for a story about aliens in Washington. I found nothing, but I worried.

I still had six capsules left. I went out drinking again, and I took them, and I offered them to girls I met for twenty bucks. They all looked at me as though I was crazy, and most of them went and sat at other tables.

I did that four nights in a row. It was discouraging. Everyone loved big tits and I could get them, but nobody would believe me. I didn't blame them. It sounded stupid.

On Saturday night I sat at a table, alone, nursing half a beer. I'd decided to finish it and go home. A figure walked up in the dim light and sat down.

"Hey." She looked familiar.

She said, "Hi. I haven't seen you in a while."

I recognized her. It was Scheherazade. "Sherry! How are you?"

She smiled. "I'm not selling beer any more. I hear you're pushing pills."

"I was. I think I'm going to quit. Nobody's buying."

"I am."

I said, "You don't need them." She wasn't enormous, but she had a nice pair. "Anyway, nobody thinks they'll work."

She waved down a waitress and asked for a beer. "I saw you with your girlfriend. I'm convinced."

I said, "Anyone can have huge boobs."

"Not anyone can be pale green. Your girlfriend was an alien, or a genie or something, and she didn't have *any* tits the first time I saw her."

The waitress came and set a glass of beer down, and Sherry paid her. She added, "If there's a way to get big boobs I'll buy it. You're asking twenty?"

"You helped me carry beer in the rain." I fished the plastic bag out of my inside pocket and gave her one. "No charge."

She slid two twenties across the table to me. "That's too cheap. Give me two. If you asked for a hundred each, people might listen."

I opened the bag again and gave her another. "Take them a week apart. Make sure you're not too big before you use the second one."

She said, "I'm an adult, except for wanting great big boobs."

"They'll suit you."

She drank half her beer and set it down. "I hope so. Really I don't care." She stood up and walked toward the exit. "Keep in touch."

I went home to bed. The next day I ordered ten thousand empty capsules and had them sent to my house.

I spent the next five days watching the sky and scraping lichen into plastic boxes with a credit card. It was tedious work and I didn't get much, but it didn't take much to fill a capsule. On Wednesday I went shopping and bought a thousand small plastic bags. I was going to get business cards made to put in them, but the man behind the counter said, "We can imprint those, if they're for a business."

"Can I have them by Friday?"

"Three days? No problem."

I got my phone number and a tiny graphic of a girl with big tits, done in shocking pink. The picture cost ten bucks extra. When I went in on Friday morning he apologized and said they weren't ready, but he'd have them by four. I walked in just before he closed, and they were done, completely professional, slightly fly-by-night looking, believable. I was delighted. I went home and put a pill each in twenty of them, and had a nap. At nine I walked into the bar.

This time was different. Sherry sat at another table, surrounded by admirers, her large chest sticking proudly out, and every few minutes a girl would come over and buy a capsule. I'd decided to raise the price to fifty dollars, but if they didn't have it I charged them twenty and swore them to secrecy. I was sure it was worth it for the advertising.

When I'd sold all twenty capsules I waved to Sherry and went home. Several of her friends looked disappointed. I watched a movie and made more capsules, and I put each one in a bag.

I did the same thing on Saturday, and I sold thirty-five pills.

I didn't go into town until Wednesday. I looked around, wondering if I could spot any of my customers, but it had only been a few days. The girl behind the till at the grocery store had a fairly nice rack, and she smiled at me, but I didn't recognize her.

I got home at about two, and I went back to scraping lichen. By four I'd harvested all I thought I should, and I was showering dust off when someone knocked at the door.

Two girls stood there, younger than Sherry. They were both skinny and cute and flat. One looked shy, and the other said, "Hi. Are you the guy who sells the pills?"

Her friend blurted, "For big boobs."

"Yes. Forty bucks each."

She held out a wad of cash. "We'll take ten."

"That's way too many. You can only take one a week, and you have to stop and look at yourself each time before you do the next one."

The first one said, "No, we're having a boobs party. We all get drunk and take them together."

I said, "Okay. But only one at a time. Have another party in a week and do another one. Okay?"

"Yes." She nudged her friend, who nodded.

"Promise?"

"Yes." She paused. "We promise."

I wondered if this was going to be an ongoing thing. I'd seen the lust in their eyes. They'd be back. I made a note to have some warnings printed on the next lot of bags.

The next day three women came, looking around as though they were afraid someone would see them. I had to stop work each time. I started to wonder if I should hire a secretary.

On Friday I took a hundred pills and sold forty. The woman who took the cover charge at the door stood straight up to show off her large breasts. Her shirt was tight across the front. She smiled and let me in for nothing. I gave her another pill.

Sherry wasn't there, but one of her friends came and hugged me, making sure I felt her breasts. She asked for another pill for Sherry, and I gave her one and refused her money.

On Saturday I tried a different bar. I'd expected to be ignored, but half a dozen women bought pills. One got five. Another asked if I took credit cards, but I didn't. I gave her two on credit.

On Sunday I slept in, and a slight, pretty woman woke me up at ten. For a minute I thought it was Scree, and I was filled with a mixture of lust and horror, but she was a stranger. She bought four pills.

I went to get a beer. It was too early, but I'd got into the habit of having one beer with breakfast. The fridge was empty.

I made coffee and sat on the steps, and I thought of fucking Scree on the front lawn in the dark. I'd wished I had a Tiki bar to entertain her, and now I was spending half my time in bars. I was making money, but not as much as the people who owned them.

The lichen took about two hours a day to scrape off the rocks, and another couple to put in capsules. I had to sell them on the weekends, but I had free time.

On the side of the property away from the road was an old Quonset hut, set back in the trees. It had come with a derelict tractor and a few piles of trash. I'd meant to deal with it but had never needed the space. I put the tractor on the 'for sale' bulletin board in the local farm store. A bearded man in green coveralls came and bought it the next day, and he paid my asking price without trying to bargain. He'd brought a girl far too young to be his wife, and she helped load it on the trailer.

She said, "You're Sherry's friend."

"Yes."

She wore coveralls, too, but hers looked stylish, mostly because they were dangerously tight across her chest. She tried to talk to me, but her father kept her close to him. I knew what she wanted, so I put a bag with a pill on one side of the trailer where she could see, and she pocketed it and smiled at me.

The next day she and a friend came with the same truck and hauled away my trash. The friend had blonde hair and was chunky, and she already had big breasts. She swallowed the pill I gave her, and she looked happy. I wondered if I'd set off some kind of contest. I told myself that the competition for mates always had been harsh.

I didn't do anything with the space for weeks. I had no idea how to set up a bar. I pressure-washed the floor and I picked up half a dozen old tables and a pile of chairs at a farm auction. There it remained.

As time went by I got busy, and I forgot to watch for aliens, sometimes for days at a time. Eventually I stopped completely. I missed trying to make every day into a party, endless sex, and having a lover with impossibly huge breasts. After a while I missed having any kind of lover. When I went to the bar I was surrounded by busty girls, but if I screwed one it would because I was her dealer, not because she liked me.

When I walked around town I could spot my customers by their bulging shirts. Women pointed me out to each other and smiled. It still didn't get me laid. I'd raised the price to a hundred dollars a pill. Nobody complained.

One day I got a phone call. A woman in another city wanted a pill, and one for her sister. She spoke in an urgent whisper, as though she didn't want someone in the next room to know. She gave me a credit card number.

The next morning I put on decent clothes and went down to my bank. They acted as though they'd done this endless times before, and they set me up with a business account and showed me how to take credit cards. The woman who helped me smiled and stuck out her chest at me. Buttons pulled tight in their holes. I couldn't remember selling her a pill. This was getting serious.

I composed a list of things I wanted in a girlfriend, and I realized I was describing Scree. I tore it up and started again. She had to not be part of an alien cult. She had to be skinny, pretty, and she had to have enormous breasts. Scree had ruined me for other women. I didn't care.

I went and filled capsules and put them in bags. Two hours later I realized that it didn't matter if my new girlfriend had big tits. I could deal with that. She just had to be okay with them being impractically huge.

I wasn't sure how many women were like that. Most of the ones in the bars stopped after one pill, but there were a few who bought a second one, and a small number on their third. None were as big as Scree.

Over the next week I sold sixteen pills over the phone. It took time to take the order, address the padded envelope, drive to the post office and pay to mail it. That got in the way of scraping lichen and filling capsules, and I was trying to do something with the Quonset hut and still make it to the bars to sell pills. I had a constant trickle of women coming to the house, and that took time, too, and interrupted whatever else I was doing. I was afraid someone would see me scraping powder off the boulders and realize what was going on.

I needed to be serious. That meant I needed help. I'd have to hire someone.

I often met Sherry in one bar or another, and she still sent me customers. She didn't dress revealingly, and I was sure she'd wanted big breasts for herself, not to attract a boyfriend, but they were huge. We were always friendly, and sometimes I felt as though her dark eyes were telling me something I didn't understand.

I decided to see if she was interested. I hadn't made up my mind to hire her, but maybe she could recommend someone.

I didn't see her in the bar that week, or the next. By then my rocks were completely covered with lichen, and I was spending too much time scraping it off into a glass jug and hand-filling pill capsules with a teaspoon. My back was sore from bending over to get the stuff at ground level, and I was behind on sending out pills in the mail. I stayed up late every night writing out bills by hand.

I drove into town and bought a case of beer, and I casually asked the guy behind the till if he knew where she was. He said she'd quit months ago, but she was working in a deli off the main street. They sent me to a convenience store, and after that I traced her to a dry cleaners.

She was there. She didn't look happy.

"Hi, Scheherazade. Where have you been?"

She looked up and smiled. "Here. The other girl quit, and they asked me to work nights on the weekends. Who does laundry on a Saturday night? I'm the only person who'll fold clothes for minimum wage."

"Do you like it?"

She made a face. "I haven't got fired yet. My median time at a job is three weeks. I instinctively hate being told what to do."

I said, "I'm thinking of hiring someone. I can't keep up by myself."

"Is this giving girls huge boobs?"

I said, "Yeah, but that might be a problem. You'd be working with the stuff I put in the pills. I don't know if it works if you just get it on you."

She said, "That's okay. I can just eat some."

I'd meant that the other way. "You're already pretty big."

"I couldn't afford another pill. It's hard to live on minimum wage."

"Couldn't you -" I decided to be honest. "A girl with your boobs could make a lot of money as a waitress."

"It took four days. I slugged a customer."

"Oh." I pulled a bag out of my pocket. "Why didn't you ask me? Here."

She beamed, and she opened it and swallowed the capsule. "Thank you."

That hadn't gone the way I expected. "But do you want a job? I'm not sure I can make this work. I'll pay minimum wage and I'll guarantee it for a month."

"And more pills if I want them?"

I knew that wasn't a good idea, but she was pretty and busty. "Yeah. Sure."

She took off the stained apron she was wearing. "When do I start?"

I said, "We could go and get lunch first."

"Are you hitting on me?"

I wanted to, but we were friends and now she was my employee. "Can we do that later, when we see if this works?"

She said, "If you fire me I probably won't speak to you."

"That's a good reason not to dive into this."

"When my boobs get big enough you won't be able to resist me."

I said, "Then if I fire you, you have to go on a date with me."

"If I agree to that you'll fire me the first time you get horny."

"Then you have to go on a date with me when I ask. But I won't for at least three weeks."

"You're assuming that you'll get laid on the first date."

"You'll need someone to show your boobs off to. We won't get a lot of customers walking in to the shop."

"You're not the only guy I know. And I can show them off to girls, too. They're more observant than guys."

I said, "Okay, I'm buying you lunch and it's a date."

"What if I refuse?"

"You don't get a job."

"Do I get paid while I eat?"

"I don't care. Yes."

"Good." She leaned forward so I could admire her breasts.

I wanted to touch them, but I was already out of my depth. Scree had been easier because I'd known it wouldn't last. I said, "Ready to go?"

She called into the back, "Al, I quit! Mail me my check."

I heard a male voice yell something angry and incredulous, so I took her hand and dragged her out of there.

We found a café and sat at a table in the window. I can't remember what I ate. Sherry opened the top two buttons on her shirt so I could see her cleavage.

I said, "So this is a date?"

"No, I'm being nice. Also I'm pointing out that being the boss doesn't make you entirely the boss."

"Oh." I stared down into the shadowed pink space between her breasts.

"Your food is here."

I'd hoped that she'd drip ketchup down inside her shirt, but she ate neatly and didn't make a mess.

When we were finished I paid and drove us back to my place. I showed her the pile of capsules on my kitchen table, and the boxes of lichen in the freezer, and then we went outside and I explained how I scraped it off the rocks. The phone rang and I dashed inside and took an order, and wrote down the details on a scrap of paper. Then two women came to the door, both looking for their second pill. Sherry took their money and gave them a pill each. The phone rang again.

She answered it and said, "This is a shit show. You can't run a business like this."

"What do you suggest?"

She sat at my table and made notes while I admired her breasts and filed capsules.

The next day I rented a truck and drove a hundred miles into the city. I found a garden center and bought five dozen concrete troughs, rectangular things with walls four inches high. It took two men with a forklift an hour and a half to load them for me.

When I got home another man was unloading a huge roll of transparent plastic off a flatbed truck. Sherry signed for it. She could have written anything, because he didn't take his eyes off her chest until his truck was out of sight.

I asked, "Sherry, what is this and how are we paying for it? I'm not very rich right now."

"Relax. I got you a line of credit at the bank. Remember Aggie, the manager?"

"Yeah. Grey hair, tall, severe looking."

She added, "Tits so big she can't use a keyboard."

"Oh. I guess that's my fault."

"If you ever want a tall, grey-haired lover, she'd be delighted."

"Is she cute?"

"If you do I'm out of here."

Another truck pulled up, towing a trailer with a backhoe on it. They unloaded it and drove away.

I said, "Teenage daughter with dreams of grandeur?"

"Flat-chested wife who won't know what hit her. But she's pretty. She can handle it."

I helped her drag the plastic behind the house with the backhoe, and when I'd got the hang of it I moved the rocks beside it. The grass beside the house was getting trampled, but I loaded the troughs into the bucket on backhoe four at a time and stacked them beside the boulders. Sherry had a big propane blowtorch and she scorched the earth where the rocks had sat in front.

We unrolled the plastic, pulling it over the rocks with a lot of difficulty, and staked down the edges. It covered most of the back yard. Sherry read the instruction sheet and installed a bank of five blowers. When she turned them on it puffed up into a huge transparent bubble with the lichen-covered rocks inside.

By then it was getting dark. I gave Sherry a ride home. She sat in the car, tired and quiet. I tried to watch her breasts shake as we went over bumps, but she frowned at me and told me to keep my eyes on the road. Then she smiled at me, and when she got out she came round to my side of the car, bent over so they hung below her, entrancing, and said in a breathy voice, "Goodnight, boss."

I said, "Want to go and get a drink?"

"Yes, but I'm half asleep. Tomorrow." She walked up to her place. She didn't have Scree's ass, but she looked very good from behind.

The next day I got up early and made coffee, dressed decently and waited for Sherry. We were formal with each other, as though we didn't know what our relationship was. We worked until noon, but by then we were too tired and sweaty to go for lunch, so we had a beer each and sandwiches and kept going. Sherry had worn slacks and a blazer, but it was warm in the bubble, and she left that outside. By two she'd shed shoes and socks, and then she made me turn my back while she took off her bra. Her breasts moved and wobbled inside her tight shirt, like pink balloons full of whipping cream, and I had to turn my back on her to get anything done. By three she'd ditched her pants and was working in her underwear.

I dragged the troughs into reasonably neat rows, and I brought wheelbarrow loads of smooth rocks from the pile I'd found behind the Quonset, and dumped them by the boulders. Sherry rinsed the dirt off them, rubbed one end of each one on a boulder and put them in the troughs, a single layer in each.

By the time we were finished I'd ditched my shirt and I was dripping with sweat. We'd only had three customers come to the house, and I couldn't face the orders. I told Sherry we were done for the day and I drove her home.

She said, "Can I sit in the back seat?"

"Sure. Why?"

"It's cooler back there."

We talked as I drove, and I dropped her at home ten minutes later.

She said, "Just a minute." When she got out of the car her shirt was on backwards.

I tried to speak and couldn't.

She giggled. "I had to cool my boobs off, but I didn't want you to drive into a tree. Thanks! Night!" She ran into the house, bouncing enormously.

In the morning I was sitting in the bubble watching the lichen spread, when Sherry came in, this time wearing shorts and a shirt she'd cropped so high I could see the undersides of her breasts.

She said, "I'll keep track of how often we can scrape the rocks. We can make a schedule. You'll have to get a postage meter. And you must have a computer round here. We need to set up a proper billing system, and online ordering. We can't do everything by hand."

"Okay. Can you arrange that?"

"Sure. But baby, I mean boss, we'll need someone else. We should have someone to answer the phone and deal with people who come to the house."

I'd seen that coming. "Do you know anyone?"

"I used to work with a nice girl. Amy. I'll get her to come for an interview."

I didn't know how to interview someone. Amy was shorter than Sherry, neatly dressed, and polite. I liked her, so I hired her and told her to start the next day.

She said, "Will I be working with lichen?"

"No, you don't have to."

"Can I if I want? I'd really like to have big boobs."

"Oh. Sure. You and Sherry can alternate days in the tent. But tell Sherry to get some filter masks. I think we should limit the amount of dust you breathe." She looked disappointed, so I said, "If that works too well you can have some pills."

She nodded and smiled. "I know it's my first day, but can I have half a dozen?"

"No. You can have one in a week if nothing happens. And if you get too big to work I'll fire you. For your own good."

She said, "All right. One a week."

It only took a few days for the rocks to turn yellow with lichen, and soon after that it spread to cover the troughs. I made the girls wear masks while they were inside the bubble. It helped a little, but within a week Amy had small, pretty breasts, and in two she had large ones. I tried to ignore them.

Sherry and I flirted, but having Amy around stopped us from being too obvious or tearing each other's clothes off, and we were too busy to do much else.

Amy wasn't good at paperwork, but she was careful and methodical with lichen, and she happily filled capsules and sold them to women who came to the house. I got another desk and put it by the front door, and she sat in a tight shirt and looked sweet and increasingly top-heavy.

Sherry insisted that they alternate days in the bubble. I knew she didn't want Amy to get bigger than her. I was worried that she'd start to feel freaky, as Scree had, so I complimented her every morning. I realized that was flirting, but once I'd started I couldn't stop. When Amy heard she stuck her chest out and looked expectant. I couldn't ignore her, so I said, "You're looking good, Amy."

She beamed at me and didn't reply. The next day she came in wearing a shirt so tight I was surprised she could breathe. Her breasts rose and fell, more majestic than sexy.

One hot, cloudless day Sherry came out of the bubble, her shirt soaked with sweat.

It had grown increasingly tight until she'd taken the scissors out of my desk and cut it from the neck halfway down the front. Her breasts stood out inside it, not spherical like Scree's but enormous fat torpedoes, firm and tanned, and covered with beads of moisture. "Shit, it's hot in there." She collapsed into the chair on the other side of my desk and fanned herself with an invoice. "Can I have a beer?"

I didn't want us to start drinking at work, but she looked as though she might pass out. I was sure her huge breasts made it harder for her to take the heat, but I didn't say that.

I got us each a bottle from the fridge, and called Amy to have one. She wasn't as hot, because she'd been inside filling capsules instead of moving rocks in the sun. She wasn't quite as big, either.

Sherry said, "Thank you. I may live." She took a long drink, and for a second she could have been Scree, drinking beer in the sun, immensely busty. I shook my head and she was herself again.

Amy said, "I can take over in the bubble."

"It's okay." I thought for a second that Sherry was going to pour the rest of her beer into her cleavage, but she set the bottle down, took hold of the cut edges of her shirt, and tore it down the front. It came completely in half. Her breasts, free of constraint, bulged out further and settled slightly down under their weight.

I goggled at them. Scree had been pretty, but Sherry was more slender, and her breasts were enormous and erotic, almost too big for the rest of her.

She said, "Crap. I only wanted to open it a bit more. Fuck it." She leaned forward, squashing her breasts into her legs and pulled it off. As she sat back they lifted and pointed at me, gloriously huge, perfect. "I'm sorry, but that's so much better." She sighed and raised her beer to her lips.

I stopped trying to think. I'd never seen anything so unconsciously sexy. I stood up and reached over the desk, tilted my beer and poured it over her breasts. Beer splashed down into her cleavage, made a tiny lake and drained away. Rivulets ran down the big curves to the outside and dripped off onto the floor.

She shrieked, "That's cold! Shit!" Then she sat back and smiled at me. "Mm. Okay, that's nice. I feel better." Her nipples stuck out. Xerxes' label had said the lichen would make them big, but I'd never noticed how huge her areolas were getting. They were like little hubcaps.

Amy looked at me, and she pulled her shoulders back, inviting, but if I did that to her I wouldn't be coming on to Sherry, I'd be an idiot. If she hadn't been there I'd have tried to kiss Sherry and fuck her on the desk. Amy smiled as though we shared a secret.

Sherry sat up straight, and poured her last sip of beer over her breasts. She frowned at Amy. "Don't. You have to work inside. We don't want the house smelling like a brewery.

Amy set her bottle down, disappointed.

Sherry looked indecisive. I wondered if she wanted to say something she couldn't because we weren't alone. She said, "If you're out of beer I have to get back to work." She narrowed her lips for a second. "I'm not wearing clothes in the bubble. They're too hot and dusty. I can take the heat better if I'm naked."

I nodded. "All right, but keep your mask on."

Amy went home at four, cheerful and busty. She always parked her old truck in front of the Quonset and waved as she backed out onto the road.

Sherry came out of the bubble when she was gone, still naked. "I'm pretty much cooked."

I said, "Why are you still here?"

"Just finishing up a few things. I wanted to show you a couple of changes I made to the computer."

She stood so I could sit down and see the screen, and she bent over and took the mouse. Her breasts hung beside me, enormous. They seemed to be bigger every time I looked at her. I wanted to reach up and squeeze one, and I could picture their warm solid weight. She moved forwards and nudged me with the left one. "Oops. Sorry. It's awkward when your tits are this big. But do you think this is a good idea?"

"Yes, it's great." I had no idea what she'd shown me. I got up, feeling foolish, and sat on the couch. She came with me, and we sat side by side, carefully not touching, stuck in a rut after months of careful flirting and work. I wondered how I'd got Scree into bed the day we'd met, and months later I couldn't make myself touch Sherry, who I desperately wanted.

Sherry said, "She's cute."

"Yeah."

"And she has huge tits."

"Yeah."

"But not as big as mine."

"No. Not at all."

A flicker crossed her face, sudden doubt. "Do you like mine? Sometimes I see myself in the mirror and they're ridiculous. I keep telling myself I won't take any more stuff, but it gets in around my mask, and I don't mind." Her mouth turned down and she looked away. "You know how it is, you start doing something and you can't stop, even if it's stupid and nobody else wants you, and you know that." She held her nipples for a second, her fingers not remotely covering her huge breasts, and she crushed them against her chest. They overflowed her hands, staggering. "I guess I'm kind of an idiot to do this. I just have this thing. I want to have huge jugs."

I said, "Amy's not light and delicate either. She looks like an icebreaker."

Sherry smiled and let go of her breasts. "Two icebreakers. Pink ones."

"We never go to the bar any more. All we do is send out packages and have people come to the door."

She made a face. "I'm scared of what people will say. I know I look ridiculous." Her hands cupped them again, and fell to her sides.

"I think you look perfect." I tried to think of something more convincing. "You need a new shirt. A nice one."

She smiled. "I'm sorry." Her hands strayed to her breasts again, then dropped to her sides.

"I'd buy you one." I wondered if she'd keep making them bigger until I tried to fuck her. I was worried that she'd eventually be unable to dress herself or stand up, and she still wouldn't let them stop growing.

She sighed, as stuck as I was. Her breasts stuck out in front of her, and I wanted to touch them, but I couldn't. I knew I should put a hand gently on her shoulder but that would be ridiculous.

We sat for a few minutes, and then I turned towards her, opening my mouth, just as she straightened and rose halfway up, turning to face me. Her breasts hit me in the face, and she gasped. "Oh! I'm sorry."

If I pulled back we wouldn't say anything that wasn't business for a week. "Why?" I put my arms around her waist and buried my face between her breasts.

She pulled them away and leaned down to kiss me. "I guess you really do like them."

"I think you're amazing." I bit the bullet. "Want to make love?"

She bit my lower lip. "We already are."

I squeezed her breasts with my hands, even though they were too big to hold.

She pushed me back against the couch and climbed onto my lap, her knees on the outside of my legs, and she leaned back to pull my shirt up over my head. "Let go of my boobs for a minute."

I forced myself to pull my hands away.

She tossed it aside and put her hands on my shoulders, just beside my neck. They felt fiery, electric. She leaned down and kissed me. "If you take your pants off we could make this into a real relationship."

I pulled her closer, squashing her breasts into my bare chest. "I'd like that, but I can't let you go."

"Me either. Can we stand up together?"

"Yes." I pushed forward to the edge of the couch, and she found the floor with her feet, her lips still on mine, great breasts pressed against me.

I reached down to undo my pants, and my fingers hit hers.

She kissed me, frantically. "We keep running into each other." She bit my lower lip.

"That means we think the same things." I dropped my pants and kicked them away.

She pushed me back onto the couch and climbed astride me, and I reached between my legs and angled my cock into her.

She slid down onto me, soft and wet. "Can we stay like this forever?"

"I'm not going to last forever. But I'd like to." I was already burning inside. It had been months, and she was incredibly busty and beautiful.

She said, "Did you love her?"

"No. I didn't even like her. She was a lunatic."

She smiled and kissed me, pressing her breasts into me, squashing them, and she moved up and down. "That's what every woman wants to hear. Do you like my breasts?"

"Oh, yes." Pleasure rose inside me, a boiling tide, and washed away everything else.

She clung to me, moving slightly so I wouldn't come to a sudden stop, and I leaned back and tried to experience her slender body and huge breasts and the dying waves of ecstasy.

She slowed and stopped, and kissed me again. "Do you always come like that?"

"Only with you. You're really nice."

She grinned. "That's three perfect answers. Do you still like me now you've got laid?"

"Stay with me."

"Huh. Four." She kissed me again. "I'm going out with a friend from out of town. I haven't seen her since last summer."

"Oh. That's good."

She cupped her breasts and jiggled them up and down half an inch. "She hasn't seen me in a year. Not with these."

"Oh. Shit. Want me to come and explain?"

"How? It's better if you don't."

I kissed her. "Take her a couple of pills."

"I hoped you'd say that. In two weeks we'll be getting orders from her friends." She kissed me again and stood up.

My hands tried to hang onto her boobs, but she pulled away. I said, "Will you come back afterwards?"

"Tomorrow. But I'll lay you when Amy's gone."

"She'll be scandalized."

She blew me a kiss. I pictured it flying over the expanse of her breasts and through the air to hit me. "She's been asking why I haven't banged you since she started here."

"Oh. I guess I was shy."

She said, "Me, too. She told me she was thinking about it."

I pictured tiny Amy and her immense breasts. "I think you and I are a better match. Don't tell her."

She said, "I was worried." She picked up the torn remains of her shirt. "Can I be your girlfriend?"

"Yes. You have to. You already are."

"Okay. Show me where you keep your shirts. I'm stealing one."

That took five minutes and another long, soft hug, and she left me, naked and erect, and drove away, leaving me alone in my empty house. I didn't mind. She'd be with me again in the morning.

The next day we were shy and careful.

Amy smiled and hugged me. "I'm in the bubble. I've got stuff to do. You'll be alone with Sherry for hours."

"Oh."

She said, "Fuck her brains out. Ninny."

Sherry took me by the hand and led me into the basement stairwell. "Hang on, I thought this was the bedroom."

"This way."

She was already topless. We stripped each other and fell onto the bed.

She got on top. "Do you mind? I think this position is easier when you have big boobs."

"Anything you want is great."

"Good. I like to feel them hanging under me." She leaned down until her nipples brushed me and swung them from side to side. "I don't know about you, but that's staggeringly sexy."

I reached up and wrapped my fingers around them, just behind her nipples. They didn't come close to reaching all the way round.

She said, "Squeeze those a bit. You can suck my nipples if you like."

A minute later she said, "I think your lichen makes them feel," and she started moving faster, "considerably more sexy. Ooh." And she moved fast, until we both came, and she leaned down to rest her weight on me. "Fuck, that was nice." She kissed me.

We lay in each other's arms for a long time, and then she asked, "Can I have a beer?"

I got her one, and we shared it, and she lay on her back, holding her breasts with her hands, and I fucked her. After that I was drowsy, and I slept for a while. Sherry woke me up with her fingers and her lips, and I was inside her and starting to feel the urge to move fast when Amy knocked on the door, quietly. "Guys? I'm going home. I'll see you tomorrow."

Sherry made a strangled noise and she pulled herself up to kiss me and fell back.

I said, "Okay. See," and I managed, "you," before I couldn't speak.

I heard her giggle and her soft footsteps walked away. A minute later her truck started and drove off.

Sherry smiled up at me. "I need a ride into town."

"Okay. Why?"

"Because you're my boyfriend and you like doing favors for me. Also my boobs are getting too big. I don't like to drive."

I said, "You could stop."

She said, "I'll have to. Tomorrow."

I drove her home, feeling happy and domestic. She got out, came around to my window, and bent down, resting her breasts on the window frame, and then couldn't get her face past them. "Oops. I guess I'm kind of bigger than I thought." She leaned down further and kissed me.

I said, "How are you getting your car back?"

"If you come and get me in the morning we can have coffee before we go to work." She stood up. "I don't wear a shirt at home."

I went home and did a few things we'd ignored in the afternoon, but Amy had taken care of the shipping and everything was okay. I watched a movie with a star who was supposed to have an amazing body, but I kept wondering why her breasts were so small. I'd been around insanely busty girls for too long. There was nothing I could do, so I went to bed early.

Nothing happened for three weeks. Sherry and I had breakfast together and made love, I drove her to work, and very often we fucked over lunch, getting hot and sweaty in the bubble, Sherry with her mask on, or in my bedroom, a breeze blowing in through the open window.

Amy watched the door in case anyone came to buy pills, and looked long-suffering. I started putting in a few hours in the evening to cover the work I hadn't been able to do during the day. I told myself that I'd saved the world from being terminally flat chested and I deserved a holiday, but nobody offered to give me one.

I realized that Sherry had no idea what had happened between me and Scree, but I couldn't tell her. I wanted her to move in with me, and she wouldn't if I tried to tell her an obvious fantasy.

Amy wore her mask in the bubble, and showered as soon as she got out, but her breasts got steadily bigger I was pretty sure she was swallowing pills when I wasn't looking. I was worried, because she was too small to have really big boobs, and they got larger until she looked ridiculous. When she'd started she'd casually squatted by the troughs to turn rocks over. After a while she'd sat by them, and one day I saw her kneeling, leaning forward to rest her immense bust on the grass.

I went inside and said, "Amy, are you okay?"

She looked baffled. "I'm fine. Why?"

"I thought you looked a bit hot."

"No, I'm fine." She smiled. "Thank you for caring."

I went and got each of us a beer, and the three of us sat on the lawn and drank them.

Amy said, "Why don't you ask Sherry to live with you?"

I realized she was completely naked, and so was Sherry. I tried to concentrate. "Because we haven't known each other that long."

"And you're afraid she'll say no."

I glanced at Sherry, who was smiling. "Babe, would you come and live with me."

She smiled. "I'd be doing it for selfish reasons."

"Like what?"

"I can't drive my car any more. I mean, I could, but it's getting scary. I'm tired of getting dressed and coming here and getting undressed. When I go home I have to change again, in case there's dust on my clothes. I just want to be naked."

I said, "You can't serve the walk-in customers naked."

"Amy got me an apron. It's just barely decent. They need to see what we're selling."

"And that's it?"

"And my place doesn't fit me any more. Most of my clothes don't do up, my tops, and my kitchen is tiny. Yours is big enough to turn around in." She turned and butted me with her breasts. "And I miss you when you're not there. I need you to tell me I'm not too big, and I sometimes need to have sex and you're not there." She tilted her beer up, but it was empty. I handed her mine.

She said, "And you give me your beer. I'm entirely selfish. If you don't mind that, I'll move in tomorrow. And I need a day off to pack."

I said, "I have something to tell you, before you do."

"You're gay? Gambling debts? The mafia are after you?"

I said, "Abducted by aliens." And I told them about Scree.

When I was done Sherry said, "That's completely insane."

I nodded. "I know. But have I ever done anything else insane?"

She smiled. "Yeah, you slept with a green busty chick. I saw her. That's the only reason I haven't got up and left."

Amy said, "My brother's friend saw a flying saucer land somewhere near here."

I nodded. "A pink one? That was Scree."

She said, "So I believe you. And Sherry, there's one other thing."

"What?"

"Where's your shirt?"

"In the house. You know I'm too big. Oh." She raised her eyebrows and shrugged. "I can't believe this, but the evidence says it's real. Can you get me on the galactic internet thingy?"

I said, "She took the router with her. I'm sorry."

"Have you given the stuff you downloaded to anyone?"

"I can't call the FBI and say I have the plans for a flying saucer. I'd like to build them myself, but I haven't had time."

"Hmm." She kissed me. "If you'll show me the stuff you downloaded I'll still move in. You're crazy, but I love you."

I said, "You don't believe me."

"I think I do, but that means you fucked a green chick and kept her drunk for two months. You sell alien lichens to girls in bars so they can have giant boobs. It's crazy that you even tried to get away with that." She leaned over and kissed me. "Thank you for not letting her make us all flat-chested."

Amy went and got three more beers, and we drank them.

Sherry said, "I'm taking off to go and pack."

I went to stand up. "Can I help?"

"No, Amy's giving me a ride in her truck. It'll be tedious. I'm mostly throwing stuff out."

I spent the night alone and frustrated, and worried that she wouldn't come back.

Amy's truck pulled up at noon the next day. I unloaded boxes while she and Sherry stood and directed me.

I frowned at them. Sherry said, "Babe, I packed, but I'm a bit too big to carry a box."

"You put them in the truck."

"It wasn't easy. It took us hours."

"Why didn't you call me to help?"

"Darling, just let me do things my own way. I can't live here and let you do everything."

When it was all unloaded we went into the bedroom to unpack, and ended up fucking with Sherry on all fours, saying, "Faster, baby!" while Amy served customers at the front door. When I came I felt lightning burn me to ashes. Sherry collapsed onto the floor and couldn't speak for half an hour, until she rolled on her side and slept. I covered her with a blanket and went to fill orders, but I didn't get much done.

Three weeks later I fired Amy.

It had taken a long time, but she was impossibly big. I agonized over what to do, but I knew I had to. I should have done it weeks back. I wondered if I should have ever hired her.

She got stuck on all fours in the bubble, and she yelled until Sherry went and helped her to her feet.

I said, "This isn't good."

She looked surprised. "It was in the bubble. I'm perfectly fine at home, I just need something to hang onto." She gestured as she spoke, and her breasts wobbled. I was sure they were bigger than the rest of her. I let it go, but I knew I shouldn't.

Sherry took over in the bubble, carefully sealing her filter mask as she always did, naked and enormous and perfect.

Amy called me. "I've lost my list of orders to send out."

"Can't you print out another one?"

She said, very softly, "No." Her breasts blotted out most of the screen, and she couldn't see the keyboard.

I found the height adjustment and raised the monitor. "Okay, is that better?"

She nodded. "Lots. I didn't know it did that."

I picked up the keyboard and went to set it across her breasts, but I couldn't.

She said, "Oh. Good." She took it from my hands and put it there. "Thank you. I'm good to go."

I looked down. The list lay on the table, hidden by her enormous bust. "Amy."

"What?"

"Nothing."

She opened her purse and took out a small mirror, and she used it to look over her breasts. "Oh. Sorry."

Ten minutes later I heard a scream and dashed to the front. She'd lost a cup of coffee under her right breast and knocked it over with the left one while she looked for it. I helped her mop up the coffee and blot the papers, and I spread them out to dry.

Half an hour later she did it again.

She said, tearfully, "I won't drink coffee at my desk again. Okay?"

"Amy, you can't do this any more. You're too big."

I'd expected her to agree, but she put her face in her hands and sobbed. "What am I supposed to do?"

I took her outside, and we sat on the front steps. She looked utterly miserable, and tears trickled down her face. I felt like shit.

Sherry came up, still naked, and whispered, "Let me deal with this."

I went inside and made coffee, and I cleared up Amy's mess, dried the bills, and got the envelopes of pills ready to mail. I looked out of the living room window, where they couldn't see me. Sherry was talking, animated, and Amy nodded. I couldn't make out the words, but I watched, admiring the enormous breasts that stuck out in front of both of them, even though I felt bad about Amy.

I went and checked things in the bubble, and moved a few rocks around, but everything was well-kept. The phone rang and I took an order, packaged it and put it in the pile to go out in the mail. Amy hadn't driven to the post office for two weeks. I should have known. I realized I hadn't seen her dress except in her ridiculous apron. She'd been driving to work naked.

I poured coffee and took it outside.

Amy smiled wanly at me.

Sherry said, "Amy's staying here. She's not going in the bubble, and she promises to not take any more lichen. We'll find something she can do."

Amy nodded. Her breasts looked like fat pink bolsters.

I was baffled. "But -"

Sherry said, "Where else can she work?"

I looked off into the distance. I had no idea. I didn't know how she still drove her truck. Maybe it had been parked in front of the Quonset for weeks and she'd slept in it. That was ridiculous. I said, "Amy, you were a waitress once." The idea had popped into my head, and it was too late to make it go away. I stood up. "Come with me."

Sherry stood up and took Amy's arm. They walked carefully. Amy held Sherry's hand and she planted each bare foot precisely on the uneven ground. She couldn't possibly do this.

I opened the big front doors on the Quonset and let the sunlight stream in. It was empty except for a pile of old tables and chairs. I said, "This is a bar. I haven't had time to work on it, but there's water and power. Amy, could you get us some booze, and mix, and have someone build us a bar and get same decorations? I want to do a Tiki theme. If you can get that set up you can be the waitress and run the place."

Sherry said, "That's ridiculous. She can't even stand up by herself. How can she mix drinks and carry a tray?"

Amy looked entranced. "I can do this! I'll need money, and a week to get it set up. Maybe two. Sherry, can you tend bar in the evenings until we find someone else?"

Sherry looked down at her immense breasts. "I don't know. I can try."

I said, "We'll all go into town tomorrow and buy some nice shirts."

Amy was already pacing off distances and dragging tables into place, top-heavy and awkward and determined.

I said, "I think we're done for the day."

Amy looked over her shoulder. "I'm going to keep going for a while. Can you get me a tape measure, and a clipboard with paper? And a pencil."

Sherry got them, and we set up a table and had a beer each while

Amy drew diagrams and made lists of supplies. I leaned across to kiss Sherry, and my hands found her breasts and stayed there.

She leaned into me. "Fuck. Take me."

Amy said, "I'm ignoring you."

I dragged Sherry outside and lay her on her back in the long grass beside the old metal building, and we fucked in the last patch of sunlight. I matched the speed of my thrusts to the sway of her breasts so I could watch them wobble. She tried to hold them with her hands. "Speed up, you bastard. I know what you're doing."

I did, carefully, and she thrust and panted until she was sweating. I didn't let us go too fast, and she fought me, but I was bigger and I didn't have her enormous, heavy breasts to move. Her breath came in ragged gasps and I could feel her tiring, and she said, "Oh. Fuck," and shuddered, thrusting unevenly, her nipples bulging out like halves of softballs.

Heat rose inside my legs and spread to consume me. The afternoon breeze blew over our naked bodies, and I felt myself disintegrate into a million glowing points of pleasure. They rose into the air, burst and dissipated.

I slowly condensed back into myself. I was lying on Sherry's huge breasts as though she was a mattress, still thrusting gently, and she had her eyes shut and sighed.

Amy said, "I've got everything planned out. Listen."

I felt myself blushing. "Amy."

She smiled. "You make these sweet little whinnying noises when you come. Sherry, if you ever get tired of him, I'd like a turn."

Sherry lifted her hips into mine. "I'll let you know."

Amy detailed her plan, and by the time she was done I was halfway to coming again. She sat and watched. "I love this."

Sherry said, "Don't get ideas." Then she sighed, arched her back, and came, and I followed.

Over the next two weeks Amy ordered supplies and designed the layout. Two local guys came and built a bar, and they varnished it and put trim on and ran plumbing and drains inside. An electrician hung lights from the ceiling and Amy stood precariously on a table and installed paper lantern shades. She bought more tables and got the local lumberyard to chainsaw half a dozen huge Tiki figures out of tree trunks, idols from religions that never existed. A truck pulled up and unloaded tall palm trees in pots, and she found grass matting and glued it to the metal walls.

On the last evening before we opened a cube van came and filled our three new coolers with beer, and stocked the shelves over the bar with booze. Sherry and Amy drove into town, new white shirts draped like tents over their breasts, and they bought juice and pop and everything they could think of. While they were gone I got a brush and an old can of white paint and wrote the names of the gods on the statues Ra, Ed, Cindy, and all the rest. I wondered if anyone would ask the palm trees for giant boobs. Then I got out a box of colored chalk and put a drink list on the blackboard we'd mounted beside the door. The company bank account was nearly empty, but we had orders to fill. If the bar worked out we might even make money.

Sherry and Amy came back, and Sherry and I sat at the bar and flirted while Amy painstakingly unloaded supplies and put them away.

I said, "Hey! Busty chick. Could we get two beers?"

She opened them, and one for herself. I smiled at Sherry. It was perfect. The small overhead lights glowed and the fridges hummed, and Amy stood behind the bar and looked happy.

She'd taken off her shirt and wore a bikini top bigger than I'd imagined you can get, a red and orange thing, huge cups that covered only the outer third of her massive breasts, and tiny straps that stretched back over her shoulders, as taut as bowstrings.

I gave her a credit card, and she solemnly rang up our bill, and I added a tip. She said, "Thank you. You're our first customers." Then she walked out to the sign board and added, 'Big Tits - $25.'

Sherry and I got tipsy and tried to make love in Amy's truck, but I was too tall and her breasts were too big and awkward, so we did it in the bushes on our front lawn where the rocks had sat.

In the morning we were both hung over, and I wanted to stay in bed, but Sherry brought me coffee. "Get up. We're shorthanded."

"But Amy -"

"You fired her. We have orders to fill, and I have to turn the rocks, and scrape the latest crop. I think we need another row of troughs, too."

She walked out, her hips swaying madly as she tried to walk without letting her immense breasts wobble. We didn't make love until late that night, when our work was done and the bar had closed.

The bar quickly became popular, because Amy was friendly and impossibly busty, and all the guys in the area came to see her. I'd expected their girlfriends to shut that down, but when they found out Amy's big tits drink was a real thing, they came back over and over. She kept a shaker full of lichen over the bar and added a very small amount to each glass so they'd have to buy a lot of drinks in a week.

I'd expected them to complain, but nobody did. A small amount of growth made women just as happy as becoming enormously bigger, and I think most of them were happy not to be as huge as Amy.

Still, over the next few months we developed a steady clientele, and most of the regulars became busty and then enormous. It seemed to be slow enough that they weren't worried, and their boyfriends didn't complain. I'd expected the bar to be a place where men could ogle Amy, but over time it became the opposite, a place for very busty girls to drag their boyfriends and reassure themselves that they weren't ludicrously too big.

Sherry changed things at the lichen business to make it easier. She bought a machine that could fill several thousand capsules an hour, and software that let us print labels and stamps. After that the mail truck picked up our packages every afternoon.

She hired another helper, Jessie, a dark, shy girl who looked jealously at Sherry's breasts. I wasn't going to have another Amy, so I limited her to two days a week in the bubble and bought her the most expensive filter mask I could find. I told myself it was working. I didn't notice for two months that she was happily wearing a large bra under a new and tight shirt.

That made work easier, and after a few months we'd paid off the bar and had money in the bank. I'd expected we'd get rich off the lichen, but we never did. A lot of women were happy to be larger, but very few wanted to be as top-heavy as Amy.

I didn't care. I had two businesses, and they made money, and I had Sherry.

And one day, a year and a half after she'd left, a spaceship landed by the road. It was much bigger than the last one, painted red and pink, and tacky. A door opened in its side and Scree walked across my lawn with a dozen alien women, all very obviously tourists.

Scree had grown into her breasts. She wasn't the girl with big ass who'd found herself suddenly top-heavy and awkward. They stuck out in front of her, two immense round bulges, but they were part of her, casually accepted, contained in a shirt that was loose enough to be comfortable but didn't try to hide them. She looked good. A narrow belt cinched her bulging white blouse in above tight pants, and it gave her a tiny waist over heavy, wide hips. She was stylish, as though the flashy company vest was something she was forced to wear, irrelevant to her cool, voluptuous personality.

She said, "Greg! There you are! I've brought some women to see your primitive world. I hope you've got beer." She sounded friendly and confident, as though we were old friends and lovers, which I realized we were.

I said, "Scree." I put an arm around her waist and crushed her to me, briefly flattening her breasts and rumpling her clothing. "The bar is always open to you."

She kissed me on the cheek, not at all flustered. "We're ditching the old language. It's crap. You can call me Tanya."

I said, "What happened?"

"Well, I came back with big tits, and a lot of the other women were jealous. Everyone had been longing for something like that, and it was a huge fad. I was the most popular girl in the world. Everyone wanted to be my friend. It spread over the whole planet in about three days. Then huge boobs started to crop up all over the place, but nobody cared cause everyone loved them. I'm still sure it was something I picked up here." She smiled. "The company collapsed. We couldn't go to primitive planets and sell them on not having any breasts when we could barely stand up for our own. Then people started re-reading the really old history books. The old ones weren't gods, they were idiots whose ship crapped out near our planet. "They didn't leave because we were ready to stand on our own. When our technology got good enough to fix their ship they took off. They still had library books they hadn't returned!" She went on, "We're done with fixing people. We can all have big tits now, and that's better."

"That's great."

"Yeah. And I'm doing tours here for women who aren't as lucky as I was." She leaned close, until her breasts touched me, not noticing. "Do you think it'll work?"

"I'm absolutely sure it will. Why don't you bring them all into the bar and we'll have a few drinks?"

Sherry came out of the house, stark naked, enormously busty. I realized with a shock that she wasn't as big as Scree. Tanya.

They sized each other up. I thought for a minute that they were going to square off and butt their tits into each other like rams, but Sherry extended a hand and they shook. They'd misjudged how far apart they stuck out, and Scree's huge breasts squashed gently into Sherry's slightly smaller ones.

I was disappointed. I'd been looking forward to a battle.

Sherry looked down at Scree's breasts, and then her own. I could tell she wasn't pleased. She said, "Greg. Stop looking stunned."

Amy swung the big front doors open on the bar and walked over to us. It was early and she didn't have any customers yet, but she was always there ahead of time.

Scree said, "Hello. Are you also with Greg?"

Sherry turned to face Amy. "His second wife. I'm afraid we're a bit primitive here."

I heard a collective sigh from the tourists. This was the kind of thing they'd come to see, men with multiple wives who fought with their breasts. I'd have to arrange some fights before Scree brought another group here.

Amy looked delighted, and she hugged me.

Sherry hugged me, too, pulling me into the valley between her breasts. It was clumsy and overwhelming and wonderful. She said, quietly, "I didn't believe you. It's all real."

"Yeah. Want to put on a show for them?"

"No. I'm going to find my grass skirt." She added, "Amy. Go run the bar."

Amy looked longingly at me, but Sherry had spoken.

I said, loudly, "If you'll all come with me we can relax and have a drink." Aside, to Amy, "I hope you've got lots of beer."

"We just got a delivery."

"Good. Set up a dozen beers and dose them all with lichen. Make it good."

"Boss, what are you doing?" She reached up to cup her huge breasts. That seemed to mean she was nervous.

The aliens looked on, realizing they were watching some kind of primitive ritual. Several of them did the same thing, laughing.

"I saved the world from the last alien invasion. This time I'm getting paid."

Amy nodded and ran back to the Tiki bar, her massive bust bouncing inside her shirt. It was amazing.

Scree said, "The girls are all here to be primitive and get drunk, and if they can get big tits or get laid that would be great."

I said, "Good. And you?"

"I'm here to ride herd on them. We had a tourist thing, but you can't expect it to start again. I'm a businesswoman now." She was wearing a bright vest with a logo on it. Her breasts stuck out enormously. "I'm not going to be your third wife." She leaned over her breasts and kissed me. They nudged my chest, gentle and immense. "Or your first. But you're still sweet." Her lips lingered on mine for a minute, and she sighed and pulled away.

One of the alien tourists smiled, appraising me. She was tall and had zebra-striped skin in pale yellow and blue. Her nipples stuck out through the sheer fabric of her shirt. She looked organized and efficient, and as though she wanted to get away from that and be primitive for a few nights. I'd bet on her planet she was middle management, and I could tell that at the depths of debauchery she'd still be trying to organize everything that came near her. I wondered if I could get her to sort out the billing system. It had got into a bit of a mess since Sherry had been running the bubble and hadn't done any accounting.

They were all the same, in various heights and colors. They all had small, high tits and the air of people who would only be here a few days. They'd looked at Sherry's huge bare breasts as though she was barely human, a primitive who always dressed that way and wasn't aware she was naked. I could tell they were jealous, taken in by the mythology of the primitive, and superior, because they had clothes and could take pictures and go home.

I'd have to order more grass skirts.

Scree was leading them over towards the bar, while I stood like an idiot. I caught up with her. "You carry those well."

She smiled, professional. "I had the spine treatment, remember? Not everything we did was useless."

I'd seen Amy move as though she was being careful of her back, and this morning Sherry had lain on the floor, her breasts wobbling above her. She'd said, "Sorry, babe. It takes me a while to get the kinks out of my back in the morning." She'd stretched, enormously, let out a huge breath and got up, carefully. "I love my boobs but they're awfully heavy."

I said, "Could you get me that?"

She pulled a vial of pills out of her pocket. "I'm prepared for that. If my girls all have big tits before we leave, I'll give you enough for yours."

"Deal." We shook hands. That would do for now, but I needed a better solution. I'd have to set aside a corner of the bar so they could use their computers to write home. If I could get on their network I could talk to Xerxes and get some of those pills. His handwriting was on the label. Maybe I'd just get Scree drunk and fuck her one last time.

Two weeks later we loaded luggage into the red spaceship. Scree kissed me, crushing huge breasts into my chest, and she pressed half a bottle of pills into my hand.

I took them, but I was being polite. Under my bed was a subspace router one of the girls had forgotten in the bar. I knew who it was because I'd seen her walk around and ask if anyone had it in their luggage. She was tall and blue, with pink hair, and she could chalk it up to vacation losses, and going home with the biggest breasts of any of the tourists. She and I had flirted, and we'd danced outside the bar, me in jeans and an old shirt, and her in nothing but a loincloth Amy had made. I'd liked her, but I was keeping her router.

I said, "Keep in touch."

"I'll be here all the time. Nobody else has as good a primitive planet." She loaded her tourists, checking names off on a clipboard. Half of them wore grass skirts and were topless, and most of the rest had shirts stretched tight over huge, bulging breasts. Several were drunk.

Amy waved from the bar, putting enough energy into it to make her breasts wobble.

Sherry stood with me, smiling, but watching Scree's enormous bust. I'd told her half a dozen times that she was better looking than Scree, and it was true, but I'd slept with Scree first, and she had bigger boobs.

The ship closed its doors and ascended into the clouds like a prop from a cheap movie.

Sherry said, "Well, back to work until the next batch." She marched over to the bubble, let herself inside and looked at me through the dusty plastic wall. Then she took off her filter mask and very ostentatiously threw it over a line of troughs. It bounced off the curved bubble and landed on the ground. She stretched, deliberately, her breasts rising above the horizontal like howitzers elevating, turned to point them at me, and smiled. Then she knelt, elaborately careful, and rested them on the edge of a trough so she could reach in and scrape yellow-gray lichen off the rocks lying inside it.

Printed in Great Britain
by Amazon

39530193R00040